# EL GATO'S VOICE HISSED
# LIKE STEEL FROM A SCABBARD . . .

. . . as he quietly asked, "Do you see why we admire those venomous spiders so much? They thought you and those *pobrecitos* would be farther away when the slow poison they had for breakfast hit. They thought I would have released those hostages before we knew we had been crossed double."

Longarm didn't like the look on El Gato's usually prettier face as he coldly added, "They thought wrong, and you heard me warn that son of a three-legged whore what would happen to his family if he ever tried any of their usual tricks!"

Longarm soberly said, "I did. I'm afraid I can't let you carry out your threat, *amigo mio*."

It got very quiet for a long time before El Gato almost purred at him, "Do my ears deceive me or did I just hear you say you might try for to stop me?"

To which Longarm could only reply, "That's about the size of it."

━━━◆►► **TABOR EVANS** ◄◄◆━━━

# LONGARM

## AND THE
## CHURCH LADIES

JOVE BOOKS, NEW YORK

This is a work of fiction. Names, characters, places, and incidents are either the product of the author's imagination or are used fictitiously, and any resemblance to actual persons, living or dead, business establishments, events, or locales is entirely coincidental.

### LONGARM AND THE CHURCH LADIES

A Jove Book / published by arrangement with
the author

PRINTING HISTORY
Jove edition / July 2000

The Penguin Putnam Inc. World Wide Web site address is
http://www.penguinputnam.com

ISBN: 0-515-12872-4

A JOVE BOOK®
Jove Books are published by The Berkley Publishing Group,
a division of Penguin Putnam Inc.,
375 Hudson Street, New York, New York 10014.
JOVE and the "J" design
are trademarks belonging to Penguin Putnam Inc.

PRINTED IN THE UNITED STATES OF AMERICA

10  9  8  7  6  5  4  3  2  1

# Chapter 1

Most likely, that experienced traveler who'd first advised
against playing cards with strangers on a train had never
ridden any Burlington night runs across rolling prairie in
a spring thaw, with the nervous engineer slowing down
for every infernal trestle and not speeding up worth mentioning the rest of the time.

Hence, well before moonrise, a friendly little game of
draw poker had commenced in the club car, and by midnight, as that experienced traveler had predicted, the game
was getting less friendly.

Things happened that way when strangers played cards
on a train, especially now that a tall saturnine individual
nobody knew had taken to winning pot after pot with a
knowing smile. But since the four strangers at the small
table near the sliding door to the observation platform had
agreed up front to nickle-ante stakes, the pots were mer-
cifully modest, and only one of the four grown men in
the game of draw poker was starting to pout like a schoolgirl losing at a game of jacks.

But a sore loser dressed cow, and wearing his Starr .45
side-draw in a *buscadero* rig, could pout more seriously
than the average schoolgirl, and as the other two losers
exchanged thoughtful glances, each knew what the other

was thinking. They were thinking that the tall drink of water raking in his third pot in a row was either too lucky for his own good, or a damned fool if he was doing it on purpose.

The younger stockman packing the Starr .45 tried in vain to keep his voice level as he suddenly blurted out, "I reckon it's about time I introduced myself, lest some mechanically inclined son of a bitch I shall not mention yet has made the fatal error of taking me for a greenhorn!"

"Has anybody around here just accused this child of cheating at nickel-ante?" the winner asked with an incredulous purr.

The sore loser replied in a louder tone, "I just said I aimed to introduce myself first. I was named Winslow Saunders by poor but honest parents. But these days I am better known, far and wide, as the Stampede Kid."

Nobody answered as the Burlington night train clickety-clacked on towards Denver under a hunter's moon. The Stampede Kid, as he'd just described himself to three grown men who'd never heard of him, smiled grimly at the older, more sedately dressed man who'd just won from him again, and declared, "I know who you are too. I heard the conductor warning our barkeep, up front, that when you were aboard this run it could mean trouble, Longarm."

The mustached individual so addressed smiled mockingly, and the other two men at the table shoved their chairs back a bit as a long, hard minute passed before the big winner quietly asked, "What was that you just called me, old son?"

The Stampede Kid insisted, "You heard me. They call you Longarm and they say you're Colorado's answer to Wild Bill and the Thompson boys combined. But you don't look all that tough to me, and I reckon *this* child could take you, if push came to shove!"

The older man addressed as Longarm heaved a weary sigh, while the other two adults at the table slid their

2

chairs quietly but seriously further out of the line of fire. The Stampede Kid wasn't glaring at either of them as the man he glared at said, "At the risk of repeating something you've doubtless heard before, Kid, you are talking like a total asshole and commencing to piss me off."

The Stampede Kid drew his Starr .45 and commenced to "fan" his six-gun the way aspiring gunslicks had been advised to in more than one edition of *Beadle's Dime Novels*.

On top of that, the self-styled Stampede Kid had loaded six risky rounds in his six-gun's wheel, instead of the safer five packed by men who knew what they were doing with a six-gun. So in no time at all the whole club car was befogged with black powder smoke as fragrant as brimstone and as easy to see through as potato soup.

A million years, or maybe a hundred clickety-clacks, went by as the two players who'd hit the floor waited to hear—they couldn't see—what might happen next. Then, as the gun smoke thinned some, they could see that the taller man addressed as Longarm was still seated upright with a smoking derringer in the hand he had rested on the table. His other hand was clutching at the front of his vest as he tried to catch his breath. The Stampede Kid had gone over backwards, chair and all, to smile up at the overhead oil lamp in childish wonder, as if he'd never seen a hanging lamp sway in time with a moving ceiling before. But in point of fact, the late Stampede Kid wasn't really seeing anything anymore.

The elder of the two survivors who'd hit the moving deck slid his back up along the window glass on his side, asking the tall drink of water with the derringer, "Are you still with us, Longarm?"

The man who'd just fired once at the Stampede Kid kept staring off in the distance at something nobody else could see as he softly said, "Not hardly. I reckon if you throw enough lead you just have to hit somebody somewhere. If either of you gents have some paper and may-

3

haps a pencil, there's this lady in Denver I'd sure like to leave a few words to."

The portly older man patted himself all over in vain. The younger survivor, shaded more by the wide brim of his pancaked Stetson, broke out a pocket notebook and a pencil stub, quietly declaring, "Why not start with the lady's name and address, old son?"

But there came no answer. The man still seated at the table had lowered his head beside his still-warm derringer amid the scattered cards and small change that had inspired so much noise.

By this time the barkeep had returned to the club car with their conductor, whose own Harrington & Richarson whore pistol was waving imperiously as he demanded, "What in blue blazes has been going on aboard my train?"

The older of the two still standing pointed at the body sprawled across the swaying floorboards and declared, "That punk with the Starr .45 near his head started it. This other gent with his head on the table finished it, but caught a wild round in the process. I think they're both dead."

The conductor holstered his own weapon and moved forward to see about that. He dropped to one knee and placed a hand to the throat of the Stampede Kid. He nodded and rose, declaring, "Dead as a turd in a milk bucket. Did either of you gents catch his name?"

The informative older survivor said, "Said his name was something like Saunders. Asked us to call him the Stampede Kid. He called this other gent Longarm, just before he slapped leather on him."

The conductor felt for another pulse as he stared soberly down at the seated corpse and declared, half to himself, "The dispatcher told me he was making this night run with us. This punk who just killed him must have been one of the train robbers he was guarding us against. I can see it all now. They slipped one on board to take out our inside guns and—Jesus, I'd best get forward

4

and tell the Pinkertons in the mail car about this! We could be in deep shit this side of Denver with the federal gun posted back here to guard that back door to our observation platform taken out on us!"

As he tore forward, the barkeep wailed after him about the two dead bodies. The older survivor, closer to the door opening to the observation platform, reached under his frock coat for a six-gun of his own as he declared in a bossy way, "Douse that hanging lamp behind my poor old head whilst I guard this way in."

He waved his gun muzzle like a magic wand as he told the younger man he'd been playing cards with to go forward and send some dining car help aft with ice buckets and tablecloths. The younger, taller survivor under the pancaked Stetson shrugged and proceeded to do as he'd been told. But as he was leaving, the barkeep asked the commanding figure by the sliding door if he was the law.

The older man replied without hesitation, "I was a brevet captain in the Second Colorado when the Cheyenne riz under Roman Nose, and as you can see, the only regular lawman in this infernal car sits dead at yonder table whilst Lord only knows what the confederates of the Stampede Kid are planning outside in the dark. So let's see a little *movement* aboard this threatened train, God bless us all!"

Nobody argued. The brevet militia captain's sensible enough orders were carried out, and there was no further incident worth fretting too much about until they rolled into the Denver yards in the wee small hours and everyone was free to chat with the swarming reporters at the Union Depot, or slip quietly away for some fried eggs over chili con carne at an all-night stand in the Laramer Street Arcade if they so desired.

It was too late to turn in and too early to go to the office. So the bemused survivor of the fatal game who'd allowed the older brevet captain to do all the talking now

5

enjoyed an extra cup of black coffee with his mince pie dessert.

When a ragged-ass newsboy came through the arcade hawking an early extra edition of the *Rocky Mountain News,* Longarm bought the paper to read as he treated his stovepipe army boots to a sit-down shine.

Longarm had been raised modestly. So his ears burned some as he read the nice things about him in his obituary, hot off the press. For try as he might, he just couldn't recall performing all those wonders. But he had to agree it seemed a crying shame that a gunfighter of his rep had been killed at last by the hitherto unheard-of Stampede Saunders. He figured he'd best get on over to the Federal Building and tell everybody he was still alive before they got to passing the hat for red roses to soften the clods as they fell.

It was still too early. But as he'd hoped, Longarm spied a familiar figure grumping along the sandstone walk towards the front steps of the place where they both worked. Marshal William Vail spotted Longarm at the same time, and almost looked surprised as he stopped at the foot of the steps to fish for the private key he carried, lest one living soul ever say they'd made it to the Federal Building ahead of him and had had to wait out front for the old fuss.

As Longarm joined him at the head of the stairs, Billy Vail unlocked the big bronze door, saying, "Morning, old son. Have you ever noticed how you can drop a jar of olives at one end of the street and find it reported as a smashed-up wagon load of watermelons by the time you get down to the far end of the street?"

Longarm modestly replied, "If we're talking about this morning's papers, the news of my death has been somewhat exaggerated. The kid credited with killing me was just a pissant who'd been reading too many dime novels and thought you could fan the hammer of any single-action six-gun and train the muzzle on shit at the same time. I don't know who that card shark he nailed with that

6

one lucky round might have been. The railroad dicks found no identification to go with an extra deck he was packing in his left sleeve."

Vail opened up and led the way into the cavernous interior as he grudgingly replied, "Don't let that happen to you again. My old woman was all weepy-eyed as she served my breakfast, in spite of the scandal about you and that young widow woman further along Sherman Street."

Longarm made a mental note to get word to more than one such Denver address that morning as he followed his boss up the marble-lined stairwell to the second floor. As if he could read a man's mind, Billy Vail was saying, "It's just as well you reported in early for a change and nobody else knows you're still alive. For I was just about to refuse an unofficial request from some political powers that be as too big a boo in an election year. I don't suppose you noticed how the opposition papers covered the appointment of General John S. Mosby, C.S.A., retired, as the new U.S. consul in Hong Kong?"

As they strode down the second story corridor to the oaken door marked UNITED STATES MARSHAL, FIRST DISTRICT COURT OF COLORADO, Longarm dryly replied, "Seems to me I did read something about a Gray Ghost of the Confederacy being rewarded for his high treason with a fat political plum, now that you mention it."

Vail opened their office for business, and led the way back to an oak-paneled inner sanctum for privacy, where he waved Longarm to a horsehair-padded leather chair near a cluttered flattop desk, then moved around to the far side to plop down and light up a dreadful cigar as he confided, "Our Commander in Chief, President Rutherford B. Hayes, has had the credentials as well as the balls to end the Reconstruction and bind up some festering wounds because he's a wounded veteran of the Union Army, mustered out with the brevet rank of major general, which is more than many a carpetbagging critic can say.

7

I know what you think of his dress regulations and his first lady heading up the Women's Christian Temperance Union. But he's given us a sound-money policy, and let us clean up most of the mess left by a well-meaning General Grant, who trusted his old drinking buddies too much whilst riding roughshod over former classmates at the Point who'd sided with the Lost Cause."

Longarm reached for a three-for-a-nickel cheroot in self-defense as he conceded, "I'm more vexed by this infernal three-piece suit than by what Miss Lemonade Lucy serves at White House receptions or who her husband has on his patronage rolls. Wasn't it old Ben Franklin who advised that politics was the art of getting your enemies to agree with you?"

Vail nodded soberly and said, "Damned right. Texas has calmed down a heap since President Hayes allowed them to reorganize the rebellious Texas Rangers, and didn't repealing some chickenshit Reconstruction rules persuade old Bedford Forrest to resign as Grand Wizard of the Ku Klux Klan and take up running that railroad instead?"

Longarm lit his cheroot, blew a thoughtful smoke ring at his boss, and quietly demanded, "What has our president's reconciliation policy toward the Lost Cause have to do with you and me, Boss?"

Vail smiled slyly and said, "Nothing to do with *me* officially. Former Confederate interests in position to return some favors in an election year have asked for someone like *you* to lead a secret rescue mission down Mexico way and back."

Longarm searched in vain for an ashtray on his side of the desk, flicked ashes on the rug, and quietly observed, "Wasn't it you who showed me that executive order forbidding this child, by name, from ever invading Old Mexico for as long as I live?"

To which Billy Vail replied with an innocent smile, "It sure was. Ain't it fortunate you're not officially *alive* this morning?"

# Chapter 2

The suspicions of Billy Vail's wife and some other older women who shared back fences along Sherman Street were not without some foundation. The voluptuous young widow of a rich old mining mogul never left her brownstone mansion atop Denver's Capitol Hill without some foundation of her own, although around the house she let her Junoesque charms jiggle pleasantly. So she was dressed for mourning in a dark silk kimono, with nothing under it, when her Irish maid recovered in the front hall and ran into the sewing room, sobbing, "Jesus, Mary, and Joseph, it's back from the grave and looking well! Himself stands in the hall in spite of thim morning papers!"

The lady of the house sprang up from her sewing machine to charge Longarm with arms spread wide, her unbound light brown hair following her fine-boned skull like the tail of a comet as her kimono fell open to prove she didn't need that whalebone corset at home among friends.

"What do you mean by upsetting us so? I'd just started sewing a new black dress, you brute!" she sobbed, belying her words by pasting her bare breasts to his tweed vest and planting a big wet kiss on his lips.

Longarm kissed her back French-style, as behind him the maid was saying in a knowing tone, "Sure and I thank yez for letting me have the day off, and it's off the premises I'll be in five minutes, if yez would care to wait that long!"

Longarm told the half-naked woman in his arms, "It wasn't my idea to get killed this morning. But old Billy and some sneaky political pals are just as glad. They want me to do something sneaky before I come back to life again officially."

His gracious hostess reached down between them to unbutton his fly as she pouted. "Pooh, that means you'll be going out into the field again, and I missed you terribly last night."

Then she half turned away to lead him out of her sewing room by his dawning erection as she added, "Let's go upstairs and you can tell me how soon I can expect you back, once we get out of this ridiculous vertical position!"

It would have hurt too much to resist. But he was relieved to hear a distant door slam shut as the lady of the house towed him after her like a pull-toy, calling him a mighty flighty excuse for a steady boyfriend, what with all that gallivanting about after others.

He assumed she meant other ladies, although he'd never offered to be true blue to her or any of his other pals of the unfair sex. So as she hauled him up the stairs by his old organ-grinder, Longarm pointed out, "You knew what I did for a living when first we met. I told you up front I was a no-good tumbleweed no sensible woman had any call to mess with. But I'm sorry about this morning's needless worry, and I don't have to leave town till later this afternoon."

She started to tow him faster as she allowed that she'd been counting on the whole blamed weekend, and once they'd reached the head of the stairs they almost flew down the upstairs hall, with her kicking off her satin slippers and letting her silk kimono fall clean off one shoulder by the time they'd barged on into her perfumed boudoir.

That was what rich folks called a bedchamber furnished with gilt fruitwood furniture and velvet drapes. Longarm

10

skimmed his Stetson one way and his frock coat another as they tore across the Persian rugs toward her four-poster. He got rid of his cross-draw six-gun rig closer to the head of the bed, and then she had him on his back across the red chenille counterpane, giving him a French lesson as she shucked her kimono and got to work on some more of Longarm's buttons. They were both stark naked by the time she forked a shapely thigh across his hips to impale herself with a sigh of content on his raging erection.

Neither had anything sensible to say as a good time was had by all, for as long as two experienced lovers could make it last. But as time and the relentless rains wear down the highest mountain, sooner or later, they naturally wound up sharing a smoke as they conspired to get their second wind, cuddled friendly under the covers instead of bouncing all tangled on top of them.

Putting the shared cheroot to the widow woman's lush lips, Longarm fought hard not to insult the discretion of his hostess or her hired help. But it wasn't easy, and he was reminded again why he spent so much time with this particular pal when, as if she'd read his mind, she passed the smoke back and murmured, "She won't tell anyone she just let a dead man through my front door. I pay a cut above the average wage for everyone who works for me, and in return they all know how long a blabbermouth is likely to go on working for me."

"The worry never crossed my mind," Longarm lied, adding, "You told me the first night I stayed over how you prefer a smaller staff than most, and only put on extra help when you're throwing a party."

He didn't add that he'd sort of wondered that first morning in this very bed how she'd come by such a desire for privacy, seeing as how she'd allowed she'd been feeling so unfulfilled since her husband had passed away. That was what refined ladies called feeling horny—unfulfilled. But he never asked her about other gentlemen callers that none of her servants seemed to notice, and it sort of pissed him off whenever she made veiled remarks about gals who slung chop suey at the Golden Dragon or herded orphans out at that asylum in Arvada. So he was proud to answer with a clear conscience when she asked in a desperately calm tone whether anyone aboard that Burlington night run had been pretty.

He chuckled and replied in a sincerely innocent tone, "Nothing in a skirt came back to the club car unescorted. I had to stay in the club car for the whole run because they wanted me to keep an eye on their observation platform. A fast pony can overtake a night train moving up on a trestle during the spring thaw."

He offered her another drag and gave her bare shoulder a soft squeeze as he explained, "Some others had heard I was on board and so, not being as discreet as anyone working for you, kicked my name up and down the length of the train until the gossip had transformed me to a dangerous gunslick on the prod and likely up to nothing good. Then a really no-good gunslick shot it out with a tinhorn gambler about my age and build, and you read the natural mistake someone made in your morning papers. How come you were starting to sew new widow's weeds? What happened to that fancy black outfit you wore to that funeral you asked me to escort you to last fall?"

She demurely replied, "I wore those things when I buried my poor husband, and I naturally saw nothing wrong with wearing the same things to a neighbor's funeral. But what kind of a woman would wear the same black dress to bury two different men who'd been . . . important to her?"

Longarm kissed the part in her light brown hair, and meant it when he said, "It's flattering to hear I'm important to you, little gal. Just let me finish this smoke and I'll try to show you how important you are to me before I have to catch that southbound combination this afternoon."

She said with a sob, "Just hold me, Custis. Any healthy man can get a woman to climax, and in a pinch she can manage *that* with no man at all. I'd be lying if I said I didn't enjoy rutting like a critter with you. But . . . I don't know, I suspect it's the way you talk to me between times, as if we were . . . pals."

He said, "We are pals. Ain't you noticed?"

She smiled tenderly and insisted, "You know what I mean. You talk to me as if I was listening as your mental equal, instead of just a plaything you had to talk to while you tried to get it hard again. Tell me more about silly old Billy Vail's reasons for scaring me half to death by letting me think you were dead!"

Longarm took a drag on his cheroot as he considered. Then he told her, "I reckon if we can't trust *you,* we can't trust the folks *asking* such sneaky favors. They say that folks who refuse to study history are doomed to relive it, and if there's ever been a wrongheaded bunch of history-relivers, it has to be the Cherokee Nation, or the Tsalagi, as they say it in their own lingo. Most of 'em speak English, even among themselves, since they were marched along the Trail of Tears by Old Hickory Jackson, with the different bands with different dialects all mixed up in the resettlement west of the Mississippi."

"Then you're on some secret mission to the Indian Territory over to the southeast?" the white gal in bed with him asked. "You've been over there on more than one mission, operating openly in the name of federal law, haven't you?"

Longarm blew smoke out both nostrils and warned her he'd not said one word about heading over to the Cherokee tribal center of Tahlequah aboard a southbound combination. He said, "I'm headed on the sneak down Mexico way. I'll be meeting up with some Cherokee in El Paso. To understand why, you have to sit still for my history lesson on a wrongheaded bunch who likely meant well, but should have paid more attention to the changes going on around them."

She allowed she'd sit still, and as if to belie her remarks

13

about just wanting to talk, commenced to toy with the hairs on his belly as he continued. "Like their Iroquois cousins to the north, along with their more distant Pawnee kin to the west, the Cherokee lived alongside running water in good-sized settlements as farming folk who hunted game on the side and made war when they had to. They were good at all three pursuits. They grew beans, corn, pumpkins, squash, tobacco, and such better than many poor white homesteaders manage to this day. They wore freshwater pearls, but hardly any feathers, and as soon as they made contact with white traders they took to cotton duds instead of deerskins. They already lived in permanent stockaded towns, and so as soon as they got their first look at log-cabin construction, you could hardly tell a Cherokee settlement from a white outpost. They were smart enough and progressive enough to take up such other white notions as ox-drawn plows and wagons, fruit orchards, and of course the flintlock rifle."

She toyed with hairs further down his belly as she demurely said that she'd read about the Cherokee and the other so-called Civilized Tribes of the Old South.

Suspecting she might no longer be as interested in talk as she'd first said, but wound up now about a tragic history, Longarm simply continued. "There were *five* civilized tribes, with the Cherokee the most like their mountain-white neighbors, followed by the Chickasaw, Chocktaw, Creek, and Seminole in about that order. The Cherokee not only acted the most white, but had the most white blood, way back before the American Revolution, with Cherokee and mostly Scotch-Irish breeds running the tribe by the mid-1700's. So you'd have expected them to know better than to always pick the losing side."

The white woman he was lecturing while she twisted at his pubic hairs now said, "They couldn't have had much character, if they let half-breeds run things."

He said, "That part wasn't so mysterious. The Cherokee were what the professors call *matrilineal,* meaning they

14

reckoned their lines of descent from their mother's clan. They were divided up in these totem clans named after such critters as deer, turtles, foxes, and such. No Cherokee gal would marry up with a man from her own maternal clan. But her kids, in turn, would count as members of her clan, not their old man's, all the way back to the first grandmammy turtle or whatever."

"Then how did white suitors fit into such a matrilineal world?" asked a woman who suddenly seemed to cotton to the notion of female family trees.

He said, "They fit in right well. Traders having good things made of calico, iron, and glass to court with tended to wind up with Indian wives of high social stature, which their breed kids naturally held on to. Since them same kids inherited their white dads' places as backwoods businessmen, along with white kin they could do business with, it followed as the night the day that such great Cherokee chiefs as the late John Ross could be as much as seven-eighths white."

She laughed incredulously and said, "That's just silly. I've heard of people who were only one-eighth colored passing themselves off as pure white!"

Longarm nodded and explained, "Had the Black Republicans made good on that promise of forty acres and a mule to every man of color, I've no doubt we'd have a lot more colored folk amongst us. During that last stock market crash and depression in the early '70s, a whole lot of gents who couldn't get a white man's job suddenly remembered they had some Indian blood and applied to the B.I.A. for a government handout. So I've met many a Cherokee over in the Indian Territory as white-looking as you and me. I reckon a man can put up with being low-rated as a redskin called Unaduti or Bushyhead on the government rolls, as long as they have him down as a Cherokee *chief*. When I first met old Dennis Unaduti, he was dressed more like a banker than Marshal Billy Vail, and come to study on it, looked just as white. He was the son of a minister and passed as white when he took part in the gold rush out California way. But he found no gold. So he came back to live as a ward of the government, or a Cherokee chief, depending on how you want to look at it from a taxpaying point of view."

She laughed and asked, "Is that who they've asked you to help out on the sly, Custis?"

He answered, "Not hardly. One of the reasons Dennis Bushyhead is a recognized chief today is that he was living off the blanket, out California way, all through the War betwixt the States. I suspect it was pure dumb luck. For like I say, the Cherokee have been a caution when it comes to reliving history. Back in the 1760s they rose against Lord Dunmore, the Royal Governor of Virginia, and naturally got licked. So when the American Revolution started, the fool Cherokee sided with the redcoats, and naturally got licked."

He moved her hand further down as he wearily continued. "Old Hickory Jackson naturally felt he owed such rascals nothing, and Governor Lumpkin of Georgia wanted Indian land opened up to the voting white settlement. So once the Five Civilized Tribes had been rawdealed out of all of their cultivated farmlands east of the Mississippi, and the Cherokee had just about gotten back on their feet out west, along came the War betwixt the States and the fool Cherokee, owing so much to Andrew Jackson of South Carolina and Wilson Lumpkin of Georgia, felt they just naturally had to fight the Union, as Confederate irregulars, and I'll bet you can't guess who won."

She purred, "Let's make love again. Those Cherokee sound like they could really use some help from someone as sensible as you, darling."

He snuffed out his cheroot to roll into her welcoming embrace as he mused, half to himself, "I ain't so certain that what they want me to do for unreconstructed Rebels down Mexico way sounds all that sensible to me."

16

# Chapter 3

None of the widely strung border towns along the Rio Grande had been border towns before the Mexican War. They'd been Mexican river crossings along different wagon traces running on up into some more of Mexico. So El Paso hadn't amounted to much until the new border between Old Mexico and its breakaway province of Texas, or Tejas as some spelled it, had followed what most Mexicans called the Rio Bravo West to where the river turned north towards its Colorado headwaters to be the undisputed Upper Rio Grande under gringo ownership of both riverbanks.

Mushrooming as a border town with all that meant, good and bad, El Paso had grown up as one brawling sprawl north and south of the river crossing. Then President Benito Juarez, kicked out of Mexico City by the French-backed Maximilian and his crazy wife Carlotta, had declared El Paso's south side the provisional capital of Mexico, to mushroom along both banks, as Republican Mexican officials and American gunrunners flocked to where the action was.

The north side of town had been incorporated as the Texican city of El Paso back about the time the Winchester '73 came out. Mexicans on the south side of the river crossing had taken to calling their own part of El Paso Ciudad Juarez, but not too loudly when *los rurales* were in earshot. Any real name changes were going to have to wait till La Revolución settled up with the dictatorship that had stolen Mexico from the Juaristas. Lest that happen soon, the current El Presidente Diaz kept an eye out for well-armed strangers who might be simpatico to ninety percent of his population. So it was doubtless just as well the local papers had picked up on the story that the well-known lawman Longarm, the notorious troublemaker known to friend and foe in Mexico as El Brazo Largo, was no more. It made blending in along the border easier for a taller-than-average Anglo wearing his double-action Colt .44-40 cross-draw under a telescoped coffee-brown Stetson.

Seeing as he was never going to get official blame or credit for the purely political favor to damned renegades, and seeing as he'd just never cottoned to the civil service dress regulations of the Hayes Reform Administration to begin with, Longarm was wearing a faded but clean blue denim jacket and jeans over his hickory work shirt, and low-heeled cavalry boots. As in the case of his well-broken-in hat, he'd stayed true to well-broken-in boots that could carry him faster on foot than he'd have managed in high-heeled Justins. He wasn't a cowhand, and cowhands only wore those high-heeled boots with steel reinforced insteps for safety aboard a cow pony during moments of frantic riding punctuating hours of tediously slow herding. Like the Mexican *vaqueros* who'd taught them their trade, most cowhands were willing to move sort of awkwardly on foot in exchange for not getting dragged to death if a low-heeled boot chanced to hang up in a stirrup at a dead run.

Longarm wore no jangling spurs for similar reasons. He was a lot more likely to sneak along on the balls of his feet than he was to manage a high-spirited mount cutting or roping cattle as tame and manageable as fat deer. A fair horseman with nothing much to worry about but riding could manage most mounts well enough without spurs. Longarm hadn't had any second thoughts about riding down to Mexico aboard his usual McClellan army saddle, until Billy Vail had suggested how much needless trouble that might cause. So Longarm had left his personal saddle and saddle gun in Denver to travel light and inconspicuously in the caboose of the passenger-freight combination he'd caught out of town in the afternoon. He got off in El Paso after dark, without any baggage or serious artillery to attract attention before he could get clear of any curious eyes around the depot.

His orders had been to get a room in the Eagle Hotel as Roger Tenkiller and wait for somebody to look him up. He knew Tenkiller was a common Cherokee name. He'd made love to more than one fair member of the extended Tenkiller family, and neither had known the others all that well. Billy Vail had pointed out before Longarm could snort in disgust that any tall dark gent with a good tan could pass for Cherokee, even among Cherokee, if he put his back into it. If push came to shove, he knew a few Cherokee phrases he could pronounce just awful, which would convince most Cherokee that they'd both best switch to the English they'd all learned once that Trail Of Tears had mixed up different bands with different Tsalagi accents from all over the Tennessee headwater hollows. Vail had been stating the obvious back in Denver when he'd allowed that a rider with a Cherokee handle would be less likely to stand out as a guide amid a gathering of old Rebel Cherokee in the old Rebel territory of southwest Texas. Vail's fatherly advice about how to sneak around near a border crossing had left out some advice Longarm was more interested in, such as just what in blue blazes the bunch he'd been sent to guide wanted to, damm it, *do* down Mexico way!

Billy Vail had told him the political slickers who'd set such a delicate situation up had assured him that neither he nor any of his own deputies would be called up to do anything unconstitutional or against the interests of these United States. But they'd added that the less anyone knew, when they didn't really need to know, the easier it might be to keep things out of the opposition papers. So once Longarm had approved the second-story room he'd hired, he locked up, put the hotel key in his jeans, and moseyed past the lobby desk without offering or being asked to leave the key with the night man. He knew as a well-traveled transient that as long as you didn't owe anything at the desk, it was no sweat off the room clerk's brow if he didn't have to fool with your key every time you went by him.

Out in the streets of El Paso things were just starting to liven up. For like most Tex-Mex towns, El Paso tended to doze during the hot sunny afternoons, and make up for lost business after sundown in the cooler shades of evening. That was when the free-tailed bats were on the wing around the lampposts and it was easier to breath in the sweet and pungent smells of perfumed Mexican candle-wax and simmering *guisado,* spiced differently in every open-air *cafetín.* The street sounds changed as one drifted with the current of the Tex-Mex crowd, with colored spar-erib venders hawking their tidbits in English on one corner, and a gal in a flamenco dress clicking her castanets a few doors along. Longarm had eaten and coffeed fit to bust on the tedious train ride down from Denver, and thanks to that really fond farewell atop Capitol Hill, he wasn't looking for a woman. He figured as long as he had the time to kill, he'd pick up a saddle gun to back up his Colt and the double derringer discreetly clipped to one end of the watch chain across his chest.

For the same reasons that nobody with a lick of sense wanted to break in a new hat or new boots going out in the field, Longarm had remained true to his six-gun and the way it rode on his left hip, with tailored hardwood grips facing forward and handy to his gun hand, whether on his feet, sitting down, or astride a saddle. But while many a Mexican out for that bounty on El Brazo Largo might have heard tell of such a six-gun riding side-draw, the same

WANTED fliers said he most often packed a Winchester '73, chambered with the same .44-40 cartridges. So seeing there was more than one way to skin a cat, or squeeze off a round of .44-40, Longarm headed for a hockshop he knew of in El Paso, just off the more brightly lit main plaza.

He entered to find no other customers vying for the attention of the gnome who answered to the door tinkle, and therefore said right out that he was in the market for a .44-40 Yellowboy.

It came as no great surprise when the gnome rubbed his hands together like a housefly atop a sugar cube and declared that it just so happened they had such a marvelous weapon in stock, at a more than a fair price.

He was lying without malice, as hockshop gnomes were expected to. The Winchester '66 or Yellowboy was the first improvement on the basic repeating rifle patented by B. Tyler Henry. The New Haven shirtmaker who'd bought out the failing company Henry worked for, and put Henry in charge of production, had of course been Oliver Winchester, a man who knew nothing about machining weaponry, but knew how to shoot, how to sell, and what serious shooting men desired in a dad-blamed rifle.

So Henry obliged his new boss by improving his basic design to where Winchester was so pleased that he named it after himself. Their Model 1866 loaded and fired the same as the more complex and hence more expensive Henry, which hadn't sold too well at forty-two dollars, or two dollars more than a top hand's monthly pay. Called the Yellowboy because of its simpler cast-brass receiver, the Winchester '66 was noticeably improved by having its easier-loading tubular magazine and barrel gripped by a wooden forestock in place of the sometimes red-hot bare metal of the older Henry.

Cheaper to make and handier to shoot, the Yellowboy had put the Winchester Repeating Arms Company of Bridgeport, Connecticut, alongside such famous arms makers as Colt, Remington, and Smith & Wesson. Chambered for any cartridge by the agreeable Oliver Winchester, the brass-action Yellowboy came to the end of its road in army ordnance tests staged in the early '70's. A rechambered Winchester '66 started falling to pieces trying to fire .44-70-360, or an extra-heavy 360-grain .44-caliber ball backed by seventy grains of powder. So they'd replaced the Yellowboy with the more famous all-steel Winchester '73 that Longarm was more inclined to favor.

But the rugged Yellowboy, favored by Indians and many a cowboy too lazy to worry about cleaning rust-prone steel, would handle .44-40 if so chambered. The one they had on sale that evening in El Paso, however, had a twenty-inch carbine barrel with its magazine only holding a dozen rounds.

Longarm used that three-round defect to beat the price down to a better price for a used and discontinued saddle gun. So they shook on it, and Longarm sprang for a spare box of fifty cartridges to show he was a sport. In return he asked the hockshop gnome to wrap his old anttique in brown paper and twine. The results still looked a lot like a carbine, but he didn't draw as many curious stares as he might have on the sidewalks of El Paso as if he'd been carrying a naked Yellowboy at port arms.

Hence Longarm was mildly pissed off when a lean and hungry-looking cuss wearing a gray Texas hat, a white cotton shirt, and a nickel-plated Colt .38 Lightning fell in step beside him to just walk along a spell as if waiting for Longarm to say something.

When Longarm just went on about his own business, the stranger let fly a dry chuckle, as friendly as the buzz of a sidewinder, before he declared, "You're an Indian, all right. You may think you're fooling your betters with that haircut and them shiny boots, but your brown poker face gives your game away, Chief. For I've yet to meet up with an Indian who's willing to speak before he's spoken to by a white man."

Longarm couldn't resist replying, "You must get along swell with strangers of all complexions. I didn't speak before you asked me to because I couldn't think of a thing I had to say to any stranger who appeals to me so little."

"Watch your mouth, redskin!" the stranger warned. "You are speaking to a Texas Ranger."

Longarm kept walking as he calmly replied, "I still don't think you're pretty, Tex. Did you have some suspicions to question this child about, or do you just feel the dirty-blond hair down in front of your big ears gives you just cause to pester gents who get out in the sun more? Who told you this child was an Indian to begin with? I don't recall discussing my kith, kin, or shit with you until just now, Tex."

"Cherokee boy, you are really asking for a pistol-whupping across that fresh mouth!" snapped the self-styled Texas Ranger. Longarm felt no call to dare the fool to slap leather in the middle of a fairly well-regulated county seat. So he just waited, Indian-style, and sure enough his tormentor confessed. "I read your name off that register you signed at the Eagle Hotel up the street. What kind of a name might Tenkiller be if it ain't an Indian name, and Cherokee to boot? Your family has a whole town named after it, not far from Fort Smith, in the Cherokee Strip, right?"

Longarm said, "Wrong. It's obvious you don't know shit about the Cherokee on either side of the Big Muddy."

He found it was sort of fun to play Cherokee as he added, in a lofty tone, "Lots of you palefaces confuse the inhabited Cherokee Reserve alongsides the Arkansas line with the Western Outlet—sometimes they call it the Cherokee Strip—west of the Osage Reserve and just south of the Kansas line. Ain't no Cherokee nor any other members of the Five Civilized Tribes settled in the Western Outlet yet. The Great White Father set that considerable chunk of prairie aside for the *future* as us fornicating redskins muster and breed. Prairie being covered with grass, and Texas longhorns grazing the same, our Cherokee Chief Bushyhead has leased grazing rights in the Western Outlet to white stockmen, seeing their cows can sure use the grassy wide-open spaces and us Cherokee the money. I'll bet you thought Dennis Bushyhead was called that because he had bushy hair, didn't you?"

The lighter-skinned Texan said, "I never stopped you to talk about your chief's heathen Indian name!"

Longarm never broke stride as he calmly replied, "You ain't stopped me. But it's a free country and you're welcome to tag along whilst I say how the Bushyhead family came by its name. In Tsalagi, as Cherokee is pronounced by the folks who speak it the old way, the family name of old Dennis would be Unaduti, which translates as Bushyhead, sort of. Dennis is the great grandson of a British officer named Stuart, who fought the Cherokee for Lord Dunmore and later got appointed an Indian agent. Some say old Stuart himself was called Bushyhead by the Indians, but that ain't the way Cherokee reckon descent. The white Stuart married a pretty Cherokee breed, and *she* got to use her dad's English name around white folks. But to the tribe, she and her kids by that Stuart cuss were Unaduti along the distaff side that counted way more. I was told a spell back by a member of the grandmother's lodge that a genuine Unaduti is a medicine chanter who wears a bushy mask of shaggy corn husks over her head and face."

"Are you mocking me, Cherokee boy?" demanded the lean and hungry-looking Texan, striding forward to block Longarm's further progress as he ominously added, "You just stop right there and commence to talk polite to a white man, unless you'd care to see just how sudden I can draw this Lightning!"

To which Longarm could only reply, shifting his package to free his gun hand, "Go ahead and draw, or get the fuck out of my way. It's all the same to me, you lying asshole!"

# Chapter 4

Folks in border towns smelled trouble brewing as quickly as they picked up on burnt *tostados* or *refritos* on fire. So Longarm and the bully had a considerable patch of sidewalk all to themselves as the latter sort of purred, "Would you like to rephrase what you just said in the time you have left, Cherokee boy?"

Longarm purred right back, "Not hardly. You're a liar because real Texas Rangers pack Colt .45's, Model '76, and sport a badge on their shirt when they're on duty. You're an asshole because neither a real Ranger nor a sensible bounty hunter would start out so rude with any man he didn't know from the Prince of Wales."

"I know who you are. You're Roger Tenkiller from Tahlequah in the Indian Nation!" tried the now really palefaced stranger.

To which Longarm replied with a chuckle, "Wrong again. For a man so free with his lip about Cherokee, you don't know shit about Cherokee or you'd know they ain't called the Indian Territory the Indian Nation since your Bobby Lee surrendered and the winning side said to forget all about sovereign status for the Five Civilized Tribes. They named an Indian agent for the Osage too, even though the Osage had ridden for the Union. So don't feel

25

too bad about my implying you speak with a forked tongue, Tex. It just seems to go with your washed-out complexion. But I got to drop this load off at my hotel. So would you like to make good on your bluff or get the fuck out of my way?"

"What's going on here?" demanded a voice behind Longarm. Knowing the Nosey Parker in the white shirt wasn't about to draw on a man's back in front of the El Paso law, Longarm turned to face the blue-uniformed roundsman and explain, "Nothing of *my* doing, Officer. I was on my way back to the Eagle Hotel when this other gent asked me for a light, or whatever. You'll have to ask him what he stopped me for. He seems a tad confused."

"Come back here!" yelled the copper badge in Longarm's ear, and as Longarm hadn't lit out for anywhere else, he assumed the local lawman was referring to the other cuss he commenced to chase along the crowded walk, around a corner, and up a darker side street.

Longarm stayed put long enough to light a cheroot. It wasn't easy, toting such a clumsy package. But he managed, and once he'd smoked a spell and nobody seemed to mind, he ambled on to the Eagle and carried his new saddle gun upstairs.

Before he unlocked the door he glanced down at the hall runner to see that, sure enough, a match stem he'd wedged into the bottom hinge while locking up was winking up at him now from along the baseboard.

So Longarm silently set his wrapped carbine against the wall, drew his six-gun, and tried the knob.

The latch was locked. As he was reaching for his room key, he heard the click of heels coming his way from around a bend in the dimly lit corridor. So he had his six-gun holstered and he'd picked up his new Yellowboy by the time a petite Mexican gal in a maid's livery came into view with a push broom in one hand and a dustpan in the other.

She slowed down considerably but kept coming as she

regarded him with big, uncertain eyes and a timid smile. Longarm nodded pleasantly and hauled out a silver dollar instead of his room key as he softly said, *"Buenoches, chiquita. Un pendejo hace pendejadas."*

"You do not have your key, Señor?" she asked, staring bug-eyed at more than a day's wages as she fumbled at the key ring hanging on her apron.

Lest she get her pretty little face blown off, Longarm warned her, "This *borracho* I know may be sleeping inside. We'd better let him know we're not *ladrones.*"

She seemed to think fast on her feet. Getting a better grip on the broom and dustpan in one hand, she rapped on the door and called out, "Is the maid, señor!" more than once before she told Longarm, "If your friend is in there, he is too drunk for to hear me. Shall I open the door?"

*"Por favor,"* he replied, casually backing her play with his derringer palmed over the brown paper wrappings of the Yellowboy.

So she unlocked the door and flung it wide to assure him at first glance that there was nobody there but themselves. He placed his load atop a dresser and crossed her palm with silver as he told her he was much obliged and sorry if he'd worried her.

She hesitated, them gamely told him he'd given her too much for such a simple chore. She said, "You could have simply gone down to the desk for your own key, no?"

Longarm nodded, but told her, "Don't worry about it. I just got paid for some ponies out to Fort Bliss and members of La Raza ought to look out for one another."

So she thanked him and they parted friendly. Longarm shut the hall door and bolted it before he hung his hat on a wall hook and lit the bed lamp to cast more light on the subject than they'd been getting from the streetlight through the window. He pulled down the blind and moved back to the dresser to unwrap his purchase. He'd have never paid for it without examining it at that hockshop.

But he'd waited until he got home to load the tube with a dozen rounds of .44-40. He balled up the brown paper and dropped it in a wastebasket. He leaned the loaded Yellowboy upright against the wall, braced by the brass headrails of his hired bedstead. Then he sat experimentally on the bed and found the springs and mattress tolerable, if only it wasn't so blamed early.

He considered going back downstairs to see if anyone had asked for him while he'd been out. But he decided against that notion. He'd just nodded to the night man while passing through the lobby, and had the cuss had a thing to tell him about visitors, he'd have said so.

That mysterious pest who'd known the name Longarm was registered under had likely simply helped himself to a peek at the register atop the desk. As in the case of room keys, the desk clerk didn't care if you did things for your fool self, and hotel registers were designed to say who might be in the fool hotel. The pest had his own pass or skeleton key too, if the match stem on the floor outside had that part right. So the Nosey Parker had searched the room to see what he might find, and it was sort of amusing to consider how little he could have found.

Suddenly, there came a rapping on the door. Longarm rose and eased on over, drawing his six-gun along the way. A traveling man wasn't required to explain a gun in his hand while opening up after dark in a strange town to Lord only knows who.

It was that same Mexican maid. She'd gotten rid of her broom and dustpan, to change into her own cotton blouse and fandango skirt of red and black poplin. Longarm holstered his .44-40 as he bade her one more good evening and added he could see she was through for the day.

She got right to the point. She informed him in a pouty voice that she was of *español*, not *indio*, descent. He pretended not to understand, even though he did. He knew lots of Mexicans. So he was used to some of their peculiar notions.

Unlike Anglo Americans, for whom one drop of Indian blood cost you membership in the white race, while one remote African ancestor made you a Negro, Mexicans held that one drop of Spanish blood made you highborn Sangre Azul, or a Spanish Blue Blood. A Mexican of pure Indian ancestry was willing to concede he might have some *mestizo* or halfbreed kin a ways back. The late Benito Juarez had been an exception, openly proud of his pure Indian descent. They said the current El Presidente Diaz wore stage makeup and had anyone who questioned his Sangre Azul family tree shoved up against a handy wall and shot for the crime of *lèse-majesté*. So Longarm followed the maid's drift when she declared she hadn't understood what he'd meant about La Raza before she'd checked downstairs.

"Tenkiller would be an *indio americano* name, no?" she demanded.

He nodded gravely and said, "Cherokee. Part Cherokee leastways. We're proud of both our Cherokee and Scotch-Irish confusion. I reckon that's because the Cherokee were a fighting breed, more proud of themselves than, say, Concho or Lagunero down where you hail from."

She stamped a foot and blazed. "I am not Concho! I am not Lagunero! I am Pima and Nedli, a little!"

Then she laughed and added, "*Ay, que muchacho!* One sees she has to watch what she says around such an *entraro*! You are with those gringo Indian policemen, no? For why are you in El Paso del Norte? Are you on the trail of some Cherokee *muy malo*?"

Longarm told himself he'd better watch his own mouth around a real breed, come to study on it. He hadn't really gotten the hang of his unusual field cover, and he'd already considered a possible slip he might have made, trying to impress that white asshole who'd stopped him outside on the street.

Longarm had noticed, talking to other white assholes about Indians, how a little knowledge could paint a know-it-all in a corner or just make him seem sort of dumb. On reflection, Longarm wasn't as certain about the way assimilated Cherokee reckoned family names. That crap about matrilineal clans was official book learning. But old Chief Bushyhead *had* bragged one time about his Baptist minster daddy, the Reverend Bushyhead, as well as a brother living white out California way, a San Diego newspaperman called Stuart. English-speaking assimilates seemed less concerned with traditions.

Longarm was glad he was packing a fake B.I.A. card. It had been easy for *him* to get her to open that door with her passkey. Wasn't it possible that having failed with that fake Ranger, they'd decided to try a woman of breed persuasion to see what she could learn about a gent signed in as a Cherokee breed?

A Mexican with a steady job in a transient hotel could be in on it. El Paso was a hotbed of border-jumping rebels, gunrunners, and soldiers of fortune. And El Presidente Diaz had kept them all at bay since '76 with slick manners as well as an iron fist. So he, or his local henchmen, would be naturally curious about any new faces in town they couldn't pigeonhole right off. And this pretty little thing was a real breed, Spanish with a hot mixture of two tough enemy tribes.

It was up for grabs as to whether the Nedli Apache from the Sierra Madre Occidental or the Pima who'd been there first were the most dangerous to cross. It was her Pima blood that worried a white man who knew more than most about Indians. Pima reminded Longarm of those quiet little gents drinking alone at the bar it was better not to mess with. An agricultural or mixed hoe-farming and food-gathering bunch, like earlier Cherokee, the Pima were much less prone than any speaker of an Iroquoian dialect to pick a fight. But once somebody picked a fight with any Pima, there could be holy hell to pay! Some White Mountain Apaches had once made the mistake of helping themselves to some Pima women and ponies. The Pima had put on no paint nor beat no drums. They'd just followed the trail of those mounted Apaches, on their own patient feet, all the way up into the White Mountains of Arizona Territory.

Then they'd commenced to kill Apache men, women, children, dogs, and ponies, after dark, as silent as those *chindi* spirits the Apaches fear, until they'd killed all of the raiders, and half of the other Apaches, before they got tired of hearing Apaches wailing all night for mercy and promising they'd never make that same mistake again.

It was said that the Yaqui left the Pima alone, and no Indians on the North American continent could say *they* were as scary as the Yaqui, who'd have no doubt been more famous had they been the ones out to keep those Black Hills along the Wyoming-Dakota Territory line.

He didn't think it wise to ask the maid whether her Nedli ancestors had captured a Pima or vice versa. He just said, *"Como se llama?"*

She said she was called Consuela, and added, "I was about to invite you to a, how you say, party? For to thank you for your generosity and because I see you are alone in a strange city with a full moon shining down on such a perfect *noche del ronde!*"

Figuring fibs disguised as truth might be the best policy if the Mexican secret service was really watching the whole blamed hotel, Longarm sighed and said, "I'd purely love to make the rounds with you, Miss Consuela. But as a matter of fact I may have visitors later on tonight. Didn't they tell you downstairs that I said somebody might come asking for me? I thought I told the room clerk when I signed in this evening."

She said she hadn't asked them anything but who he might be when she was down in the lobby fixing to leave for that party. Then she sighed and stepped back out into the hall as she murmured it would have been a swell party if she could have brought him along. As she turned away, Longarm sighed some too. She sure moved nice in that

31

fandango skirt, and he'd about recovered from that fond farewell up Denver way.

But even if he hadn't been expecting those mysterious Cherokee to contact him, sooner or dammit later, a man who let a possible agent of the Diaz dictatorship lead him anywhere along the border after dark was a man who needed his pecker examined because it was causing his brain to go numb!

He moved over by the window, trimmed the lamp, and raised the shade to see if he could spot Consuela meeting anyone out front. He didn't see her. She'd likely turned the other way while leaving for that party, if not to report in to her real job in El Paso. Longarm consulted his pocket watch by the dimmer light from outside. It was later than he'd thought. They'd had the poor little gal working until midnight. It was easy to lose track of the hour after dark where the streets stayed crowded with Spanish-speaking folks. In high summer they hardly sat down to a warm supper before ten P.M., and might be serving dessert as the clock struck twelve.

He started to relight the lamp, then realized he had nothing to read, so what the hell, and maybe there was a magazine stand not too far from the Eagle.

Then there came another tapping on his chamber door and, certain it was more likely one of those Cherokee he'd been sent to meet than a fool raven, Longarm ambled over with a smile, but drew his six-gun all the same.

It was neither a raven nor a Cherokee. The part Pima-Nedli Consuela was standing there with a shy smile, a basket of nachos, and a bottle of tequila. "I was wondering, since you can not come with me to that other party," she said, "why we could not have our *own* party *here* as we wait for your friends to join us."

He reholstered his six-gun and made sure of the barrel bolt as she moved over to the bedstead with her food and drink. He was glad they supplied a pitcher of water and two hotel tumblers with the room. A man could die washing down spicy nachos with hundred-proof tequila.

As Consuela sat on the bedstead, demurely spreading her red and black skirt atop the covers, Longarm considered lighting that lamp after all. Then he wondered why anyone would want to do a stupid thing like that as he sat down beside her with those tumblers and the chaser water to reach for the bottle she'd placed beside that trimmed lamp. As he pulled the cork with his grinning teeth, two men on the far side of the street were staring thoughtfully up at his dark window.

The one who'd tried to play Texas Ranger grinned lewdly and said, "Our little friend sure works fast! We'd barely sent her back for more when they trimmed the lamp and opened the shade as if for more air to breathe!"

The Mexican beside him sniffed and warned, "Do not speak of a most dedicated agent of my government with contempt. She is only doing what she has been ordered to do. But by the beard of Christ she does it well, and she will soon find out what *mierda* they are really up to!"

# Chapter 5

Sharing nachos and tequila on a bedspread in a dark room made it easy to get started when all concerned had getting started in mind.

But once he had them undressed and got to probing her wet warm *funciete* with his old organ-grinder, she protested it was too big, begged him not to go so deep, and proved how much she meant that by thrusting her pelvis up to meet his in a series of rapid-fire bone-rattling bumps and grinds.

Most men would have come like jackrabbits in such exciting company. But thanks to a paler and more padded pal he'd gotten excited with not too far on the other side of sundown, Longarm was able to surprise and delight the trimmer and duskier Consuela by lasting until he made her climax ahead of him, finishing with protracted efforts as she wriggled and giggled and fingered her own clit and one nipple all aflutter, gasping *"Como el amor de Dios, tienes mi corazon en tus manos!"*

So he figured it might be proper to address her as his *querida* when he managed to come in her at last.

As some kindly old philosopher had once observed, doubtless in French, no man is ever as completely sane as he is after a bite to eat and a good piece of ass. So even as Longarm left it in her to soak, doubting he'd ever get it up again if he allowed it to go all the way soft, he was aware he'd have doubtless come quicker if only he hadn't suspected she'd been sent to spy on him. Female spies had an unfair advantage over male spies on such informal occasions, able to grin and bear it with men they were downright disgusted with, while a man had to like a gal at least a little—unless he was one of those sick bastards who liked to rape gals he was mad at, and vice versa.

Consuela helped a little by clasping his semierection as warmly as a politician shaking hands in his home district. He liked her even more, or at least disliked her less, when she coyly suggested they do it some more in the manner of *los perros.*

He knew the experienced little gal wanted to pump him for information as long as she was getting humped, and as all experienced sex maniacs knew, dog-style was the most conversational position in the *Kama Sutra.* That was a dirty Hindu love manual, illustrated, that you could buy on the sly, with a plain brown-paper cover, if you knew who to ask.

Grasping one of Consuela's firm hard-working *nalgas* in each hand as he planted his bare feet on the coiled cotton rug, Longarm worked his semisoft but considerable *piton* back inside her while she told him she wanted *el todo,* or all he could give her, now.

He was willing. Moving in and out was easier when a man didn't have to lift his big ass and drop it, like a sledgehammer breaking ballast rocks.

Consuela arched her spine to take it deeper as she coyly suggested she knew what he and his Cherokee pals were up to down Mexico way.

Longarm thrust in response to her invitation as he told her, truthfully enough when you studied on it, that *she* knew more than *he* did if she knew what he was doing in El Paso.

He explained, "The reason I asked downstairs about anybody asking for me was that mutual pals asked me to meet some Cherokee folks down here in El Paso. Who told you they were Cherokee, by the way? I don't recall describing anyone as anything down in the lobby."

He had to admire her quick wits as well as her lithe tawny torso as she easily replied, "Who else would an hombre with a Cherokee name be meeting here on this side of the border, where Los Tejanos refuse for to drink with anyone of *indio* blood, unless they are young and *muy linda*? You have a big *pistola* hanging from the bedpost, with a repeating rifle for to keep it company. I think they wish for to have many well-armed riders when they cross the Rio Bravo to follow the trail of the Great Cherokee Chief, Sequoya, to Tamaulipas, eh?"

He replied sincerely, "What's in this Tamaulipas? And George Guess, or Sikwayi as us redskins pronounce it, died before either of us were born!"

She said, "*Sí*, in Tamaulipas, searching for that lost tribe of his own people, no?"

Longarm kept it moving just enough to keep it from going soft as he wondered what in thunder the Mexican secret service could have in mind. He'd heard all about the romantic legend of Sequoya, chasing a bunch of moonshiners in the Indian Territory. The Cherokee who'd told him about the poor old crippled drunk had thought the missionary version funny as all get-out.

Seeing he was supposed to be Cherokee that evening, Longarm told the Pima-Nedli breed he was humping, "He never found no Cherokee in Old Mexico. The Cherokee riding with him on his quest came back to tell the tale."

"What happened to the poor chief? Was he murdered by *ladrones*?"

Longarm snorted. "He was an eighty-three-year-old cripple in poor health when he set out from what was then the Indian Nation. Nobody had to murder him, albeit some say his demise was hastened by broken dreams. Old

George dreamed a heap. He was born before the American Revolution to a Scotch-Irish Indian trader and a Cherokee breed. He was never a chief, nor even taken serious by Cherokee kids playing around his dad's trading post. Nobody knows how he ever grew up so uneducated in a family ordering trade goods by mail and shipping hides, pearls, and pelts to the outside world.

"But he must have had a hazy notion at best of how reading, writing, and 'rithmetic really worked. For as a grown man he was suddenly inspired to invent writing from scratch, with an eighty-odd-symbol alphabet as that looked more like cattle brands than the twenty-six Roman letters the Cherokee had gotten by with. High Chief Moytoy signed a treaty with Royal Governor Oglethorpe of Georgia in English and phonetic Tsalagi in 1736. But as you Mex folks should have noticed by this time, when you don't know your history you get to relive it. So old George Guess showed his new alphabet to literate Cherokee, who just laughed at him, and then to some uneducated Cherokee, who thought he might be on to something. Let's turn you over and do this right."

She was willing, and this time, when he hooked his elbows under her bent knees, she just opened wide and said, "Ahhhhh!"

Later on, as they were sharing a smoke while the balmy draft from the open window cooled their flushed hides, Consuela brought up the Great Sequoya, or whatever he'd been, some more.

Longarm explained, "He was greater to the white missionaries who seemed to find the notion of a part Cherokee who'd invented his own impractical alphabet a thundering wonder. I say impractical because, after all the excitement of printing a Cherokee hymn book and the New Testament with expensively cast type, they went back to printing both a little Tsalagi and a lot of English newspaper articles in plain old Roman font. The reason most of the articles in the famous *Cherokee Phoenix,*

37

hailed as the first Indian newspaper, got printed in English was twofold. Nobody could agree on which of the three main Cherokee dialects should be official, and second, the publisher, Sam Worcester, and the editor, Elias Boudinot, were white men. I've won bar bets on them because they, or the missionary society backing their play, used Cherokee George Guess as a sort of front man, dubbed Sequoya as a sort of pet noble savage. Old Hickory Jackson's agents admired Sequoya too. They thought he was more important in tribal affairs than any Cherokee ever did, and he was in with the clique willing to agree to that Indian Relocation Act for a nominal fee."

Longarm was wryly surprised at how pissed off he was starting to feel about the Trail Of Tears, even just *pretending* to be part Indian. He wondered whether pretending to be hot for a man they'd sent her to pump for information had made Consuela wiggle half of those wiggles sincerely. He knew *he'd* wiggled sincerely enough.

Aiming to give the Mexican Secret Service their money's worth, Longarm continued. "Out west in the new Indian Nation, old George Guess wanted to be called Sequoya all the time, and was, in the *Cherokee Pheonix,* as a sort of Cherokee version of Hiawatha."

"Who is this Hiawatha?" the Mexican gal asked with a friendly snuggle.

He rolled a nipple between thumb and forefinger like a gumdrop as he replied, "Never mind. That legend is too long to go into, and you have my word neither Hiawatha nor Miss Minnehaha ever went anywheres near old Mexico. The reason George Guess went, as Sequoya, was that he had to do *something* new after resting on his laurels for many a year, and he'd heard gossip about some Cherokee, or some far-off folks speaking Tsalagi, south of the border."

Longarm blew a thoughtful smoke ring and added, "It's my own considered opinion that, at best, some traveler had reported on Gulf Coast Caddo. Both the Cherokee and their Iroquois cousins farther north had moved east across the Mississippi not too long before Columbus was heading the other way across the Atlantic. So such western and southwestern nations as the Pawnee, Wichita, Caddo, and such speak dialects related to Iroquoise and Cherokee sort of. Cherokee from one watershed had a tough time understanding Cherokee from another, and neither savvied an Iroquois any better than a French Creole might savvy a Mexican, no offense."

"Then these *indios* Sequoya searched for near Tamaulipas were Caddo?" she asked.

He snuffed out the smoke to screw her some more as he assured her, "Sequoya never found nothing in Old Mexico. He just went down yonder like Ponce de Leon searching for that other mythical wonder, and died of old age and natural causes."

"Then why are you and those other Cherokee planning on following his trail south of the border?" she went on, bless her firm tits and fuzzy little ring-dang-doo.

He kissed her, hauled her further down the mattress, and would have mounted her again if somebody hadn't been banging on the infernal door and calling out in what might have been Tsalagi. It sounded sort of like: *"Ogidoda galvladi hehi galvghwo-diyu gesesdi detsado-vi . . ."*

Longarm rolled off Consuela to land on his bare feet with six-gun in hand as he called back, *"Tsuli gahlv iha,* and if you don't follow my drift we'd best speak English!"

The same female voice dryly replied, "That's all right with me. If I didn't know better, I could swear you'd just said you'd tied up a bird!"

Longarm felt no call to explain about that time in Tahlequah when he'd read a tedious article about Cherokee grammar in their tribal newspaper. They could use the same verb more ways than you could shake a stick at, and all that had stuck was that *gahlv* was the root of "to tie."

He had no idea how that *bird* had popped into his head. He moved closer to the door and asked, "Who's out there? I've been in bed without a stitch on."

His late-night visitor rattled the knob in vain as she replied, "I'd be Clovinia Spotted Deer. Let me in. We have to talk!"

Longarm insisted, "I'm still naked. Why don't I join you as soon as I can get dressed and wash the sleep-gum out of my eyes. What room are you in, Miss Clovinia?"

It worked. He hadn't known what he was going to do if she'd said she'd wait there in the hall. But Lord love her, she told him she was in Room 208 and that she'd leave her latch unlocked. Then he and Consuela heard her footsteps fading off down the hall. So the petite Mexican spy was out of bed and slipping back into her duds before Longarm could think up a polite way to suggest it. She kissed him while he was still fumbling on his underdrawers and purred, *"Me maravillo que estoy vivo, querido. But I thank you for a lovely evening."*

Then she was out the door before he could finish telling her *he* was surprised he was still alive as well. So he cleaned up at that washstand in one corner, finished dressing, and left his hat to keep company with the new Yellowboy as he and his six-gun ambled out and down the corridor to Room 208.

She'd said it would be unlocked, but he tapped the door anyhow as he twisted the knob and went on in. Room 208 smelled of lamp oil and medicine smoke. Lots of assimilates dropped a pinch of ground-up herbs and worse down a lamp chimney to make their quarters smell more like home. The only figure in Room 208, standing in the center, had to be Clovinia Spotted Deer, whoever she might be.

Longarm figured it was just as well he'd had two women, both great lays, within less than twenty-four hours. For Clovinia Spotted Deer would have otherwise inspired a raging hard-on, and they hardly knew one another to howdy.

The Cherokee gal, or at least a lady with a Cherokee name who spoke Tsalagi fluently, was a willowy ash-blonde, taller than either little Consuela or the statuesque widow woman of Capitol Hill. Her big, sloe eyes and high cheekbones were the only hints of Indian blood to be seen, if one looked for any. In her ecru silk summer frock and stylish high buttons, Clovinia Spotted Deer could have passed for a Denver debutante at a statehouse shindig. So Longarm was pleased not to blush like a schoolboy as she held out a gracious hand, for a man to shake, not kiss—in a border-town hotel, for Pete's sake.

Longarm said, "I'm sorry if my Cherokee talk confounded you, Miss Clovinia. I know you know who I really am. I was keeping up my false front for someone I suspect was a Mexican spy."

The blond Cherokee gal smiled knowingly, and this time Longarm did feel a little glow to his cheeks as she calmly said, "I saw her leave, and I can see why you were naked when I knocked on your chamber door. I can't say a thing against her figure, if you like them small. But I can't say much for your taste either, Mr. Tenkiller."

He didn't look away, but it was tempting, as she stared him right in the face and added, "Honest Injun, couldn't you do better than that swarthy little squaw? Where did you ever find one that *dark* when you set out to change your luck?"

41

# Chapter 6

There were times a man just had to resist temptation. Consuela, for all her faults, was a *mestiza*, meaning she and
Clovinia both had to have at least one ancestor more Indian than either of them. But even colored folks sneered
at other colored folk who were a shade duskier. They
could make much crueler comments about field help than
any white who wasn't a paid-up member of the KKK.

So Longarm told the blond Cherokee, "I was acting
under duress in the line of duty. I just told you the Mexican secret service sent her to spy on us, and spying right
back, I found out they're on to this mission, albeit they
have it down as some quixotic quest for a long-lost band
of Cherokee."

Clovinia gasped. "Oh, no! How could they have found
out? We were assured by our friends in the B.I.A. that the
matter could be dealt with in secret by the party machine,
with no elected officials higher than the Secretary of the
Interior needing to know about it!"

Longarm shrugged and said, "You're talking about a
heap of paper pushers working for . . . Land Management,
right? Could we sit down, Miss Clovinia? I fear we have
some details to thrash out despite the hour."

She waved him to a bentwood chair, and sat primly on

the edge of her hotel bedstead as she asked, "How many Mexicans do you imagine they'd have working for Indian Affairs or Land Management, and who told you about that branch of Interior being involved in the . . . expedition?"

Longarm replied easily, "My boss back in Denver calls it a process of eliminating. None of you Cherokee folks had the vote in national elections *before* you rode for the South against the Union, no offense. So neither party machine would be bending the rules for a block of Cherokee votes."

He ran an admiring glance over her expensive summer outfit as he added, "Some few of you have done right well in your new settlements west of the Mississippi, mostly in trade or tribal politics, meaning your average Cherokee family is no richer than your average Western homesteader's family of any persuasion. So that eliminates direct campaign contributions, and what do we have left that an influential Cherokee might offer?"

She didn't answer.

Longarm nodded as if to himself and insisted, "Grazing rights in that so-called Cherokee Strip. Not direct to the party machine. But as dirt-cheap grass to cattle barons who *do* contribute to the party of their choice, which is naturally the party that can do them the most favors, and why am I telling you things we both know? I still don't know why they recruited me unofficially to meet up with all you Cherokee, and whilst we're on the subject, where *are* all you Cherokee?"

She said, "You're as sharp as they say. It's almost time to leave this hotel. They're closing up and most couples on the street right now are looking for trouble, with the Street Arabs hoping for Anglo males to be rich drunks and any woman on the street at this hour a streetwalker who'd rather give in than fight them."

Longarm smiled thinly and decided, "Someone *has* been telling you folks from the Indian Territory about the facts of life along this border!"

She sniffed and said, "Not all of us have spent much recent time on the reservation. The Pikes Peak gold rush was launched by Cherokee prospectors. Some of our savage forebears took part in that first gold strike in the Georgia. Chief Bushyhead's brother publishes a newspaper out California way for a pure palefaced readership, you know."

He said, "I knew. I was just telling that Mexican spy all that. So you don't have to sell me the Five Civilized Tribes as a tad more advanced than Digger Indians. I'd like to know what I'm going to be asked to do for your mysterious expedition, if and when I ever meet up with them!"

Clovinia Spotted Deer said, "Lead us, or guide us at least, down along the timberline of the Sierra Madre Occidental as far as the headwaters of a river they call the Verde."

Longarm whistled softly as he consulted his mental maps of the country she was talking about. It was rough country in the best of times, and these were not the best of times, so he said so, adding, "The B.I.A. stirred up a hornet's nest when they tried to move old Victorio's Mimbrenos from their favorite camping grounds along the upper Gila to the San Carlos Reserve out near Fort Apache. Victorio lit out with thirty Mimbrenos to raise so much pure Ned that eighty Mescaleros threw in with them. Last time they stood still long enough for rough estimates, he was leading three or four hundred Bronco Apache along either bank of the Rio Grande, depending on which army was gaining on them. The U.S. Cav and Mex *federales* have set some differences to one side in favor of killing Victorio, not rounding him up, this time."

She shrugged and asked, "How much of a problem should those border-raiding Apache be to us, once we're a day's ride south of the river?"

Longarm said, "Plenty. Like I said, a hornet's nest, with nobody, including Victorio, certain where he'll hit next.

44

Leaving both armies patrolling far and wide with orders to shoot to kill. With the possible exception of the Pima on either side of the border, most every Quill Indian for more than a day's ride down through the Sierra will be on the prod and loaded for bear, with armed and dangerous Mexicans divided as to whether Nedli or Yaqui are meanest, but agreeing any obvious Indian should be shot on sight. So there goes any notion of traditional Cherokee duds, and did I fail to mention how many Mexicans of various political persuasions shoot anyone they take for Anglo on sight? They're still smarting from the Mexican War and Maximilian's soldiers of fortune. So the one thing most Mexicans agree with El Presidente Diaz about is that poor Mexico was created too far from God and too close to Los Estados Unidos. That's what they call us. Do you speak Spanish, by the way?"

She said, "No. We were assured you were fluent in Spanish and very familiar with the Sierra Madre Occidental. That was the main reason we asked for you, ah, Mr. Tenkiller."

He said, "My friends call me Custis, or mayhaps Roger would be best for now, seeing that's what's on my fake B.I.A. registration card. My Spanish is good enough to order a meal or find my way to a railroad depot in Old Mexico. It ain't good enough to pass me off as a Mexican. And the reason I'm so familiar with northern Mexico is that I've been chased through so much of it by *banditos, rurales, soldados,* real wild hill tribes, and just plain mean Mexicans. So I sure hope you Cherokee in need of guidance have something important waiting for you down by the Rio Verde!"

She nodded primly and said, "We do. It's a rescue mission, funded by Texas conscience money and designed to save the remnants of a long-stranded band of Christian Cherokee!"

Longarm mulled her surprising notion over in his mind before he pointed out, "Old George Guess never found any long-lost Cherokee down Mexico way. He died looking for them."

Clovinia nodded, but said, "In the wrong parts of Old Mexico, not long after the Trail of Tears and just before the Mexican War. He'd moved out west before he ever heard of the band who'd strayed south, searching for well-watered hollows along first the Rockies and then on down through the Sangre de Cristos to the Sierra Madre. There they encountered earlier agricultural Indians where the hollows were right for the four sisters—beans, corn, squash, and tobacco. The rest was too dry to settle, until much farther south than poor old Sikwayi ever made it, they found a well-watered hollow to call their own."

She could see the dubious look in Longarm's eyes as she continued. "We're not sure how Sikwayi heard about such faraway kinfolk who were still praying to the mysteries of the old way. Some say a Cherokee prospector, searching down the Continental Divide for color, simply stumbled over Mexican mountaineers who spoke his own dialect. However it happened, poor old dreaming Sikwayi heard about it and went in search of them, in all the wrong places, to offer hymn books and Bibles to them, printed in that syllabic alphabet he'd dreamed up."

"And so he died trying and *that* dream never came true for the old man either," Longarm said with a sigh.

She answered, "That didn't really mean he'd been on a baseless mission. He died trying in '43, and the war with Mexico broke out in '46, so there went any further searches funded by the Methodist Missionary Society. But in '47, during the occupation of Mexico City, a Cherokee scout on the American side overheard two Mexican prisoners of war conversing in Tsalagi. When he asked them where they were from, they told him they'd been recruited from Tsaragi, the Tsalagi homeland early English traders pronounced as Cherokee as the English name for both a people and their lands on both sides of the Tanasi."

Longarm started to ask if they were talking about the

Tennessee River, but that would have been a dumb question as well as a distraction. So he just nodded and she continued. "The Cherokee scout from the real Cherokee Nation didn't see how that could be. So he questioned them further, and he naturally knew about the prewar search of Sikwayi. So they soon thrashed it out, and once our own Cherokee was mustered out and returned to Tahlequah, he told his Southern Baptist missionary, not the Methodists from Pennsylvania, about those still-pagan Cherokee down Mexico way around the headwaters of the Rio Verde in rugged mountains few Mexican Christians felt safe in."

Longarm nodded again, but pointed out, "The Mexican War ended in '48, and so the California gold rush and a lot of other water has spilled over the dam since then. What makes you so sure your long-lost kissing cousins still have to be there?"

She said, "We're still in contact with them, and while they themselves feel they can survive the present turmoil down Mexico way, the *missionaries* among them are in grave danger. They're naturally Baptist Cherokee from Tahlequah, but as you may have noticed, and as your fake identification would indicate, a lot of Cherokee from north of the Rio Grande can be taken at first glance for a gringo, as I believe both sides down Mexico way put it."

Longarm said, "I'm starting to follow your drift. I know how popular Americans have been since the United States Marines butchered all them young Mex military cadets at Chapultepec, to hear Mexicans tell it. It can sure be a waste of time pointing out that military cadets standing their ground whilst more sensible Mex infantrymen retreat are sort of *asking* to be butchered. But sometimes it's tough to offer a history lecture in a Mex dance hall when a dozen liquored-up *muchachos* get to muttering about gringos. But you've gotten ahead of your story. You forgot to tell me how them paler-faced Cherokee wound up in the Sierra Madre Occidental to begin with, and how

47

come none of us total palefaces ever heard tell of such a situation."

She wrinkled her pert nose and asked, "How much do you read in the *Denver Post* about American missionaries in China, or those Sandwich Islands? You've read *less* about Cherokee missionaries of the Southern Baptist persuasion because there are some things we don't pester the rest of the world about and because of that other war we had between then and now. Nobody could act upon the reports of that Cherokee scout home from the Mexican War until the late '50s, with the bigger war's thunder clouds looming over the eastern horizon. Let's not get into the night riding just to our north in the free state of Kansas, with neither side covering itself with unsullied glory as they burned each other's barns and murdered one another's women and children in the name of abolition and states' rights. Suffice it to say the Cherokee Nation, as it was still called, tried to avoid calling attention to its own delicate position as a self-ruling state within quarreling states. The national council—you call it a tribal council these days—forbade any missions to Mexico as trouble brewed down yonder between the Conservatives led by Santa Ana and the Liberals led by Juarez. It seemed an awfully confusing mess to meddle with."

Longarm smiled thinly and agreed. "The French under Louis Napoleon sure found that out when they decided it might calm things down if they installed a puppet emperor. I take it some Cherokee missionaries disobeyed their higher authorities?"

She sniffed and demanded, "Didn't St. Paul when he carried the Word to Rome? A mission was sent discreetly down to the headwaters of that Verde River, and got through with the word and a box of Cherokee Bibles printed in the Sikwayi syllabary. We imagine any that fell into the hands of Mexican Papists would have been dismissed as unreadable nonsense. The mission was a resounding success. The whole lost tribe was converted en masse. Then travel between the Cherokee Nation and a mission deep in Old Mexico got too hard to manage, for a long time."

Longarm dryly remarked, "I reckon it did, what with you Cherokee siding with the South and getting overrun by Union troops whilst all them Mex guerrillas fought the French Foreign Legion. So your mission down yonder was cut off, and then what?"

She shrugged and said, "Then they just managed to get along as best they could, supported and hidden from all Mexican outsiders. After our own troubles with the Reconstruction ended barely two years age, we were able to exchange occasional messages and help them out with some contributions. We have friends in high places with hungry cows to feed, and perhaps some lingering feelings of guilt about how we'd once all left the Old South."

She suddenly got to her feet, adding, "It may be safe to risk the streets of El Paso now. Suffice it to say, we recently got word those missionaries are under ever-increasing danger because of the current political turmoil in Old Mexico. Why don't you get your rifle from your own room so I can introduce you to the others now?"

# Chapter 7

Longarm didn't have to ask why a bigger bunch holed up in other parts of a border town had asked him to meet them at the Eagle and risked one harmless-looking scout to contact him there. But she told him they were headed for a private home owned by a Texas ranchero as he escorted her along back streets in the first hint of dawn.

Her blond hair and his recently shined boots attracted speculative glances and sucking sounds from Mexican kids lounging in dark archways. But nobody wanted to mess with a man the size of Longarm packing a six-gun and a Yellowboy.

Along the way she elaborated some on the more recent perils of an isolated Protestant mission surrounded by Spanish Catholics, Indians who were still praying to a feathered serpent, and Mexican revolutionaries who thought all priests and ministers were oppressors of the people and had to die.

There were always more bandit and rebel bands as travelers moved farther off the beaten tracks patrolled by *los rurarles,* and thanks to Victorio, that spring there were fewer *rurale* patrols anywhere as you moved south through rugged and barely mapped hill country. Clovinia said she wasn't sure which of several menacing factions was worse, but she was sure those breed missionaries were scared of *somebody,* and Longarm could see why.

Those Mexican wanted fliers out on *him* had been inspired through no fault of his own by fights he'd never picked with just plain ornery Mexican bandits, rebels, and *rurales* hunting them, who'd all seemed to agree that a gringo riding alone after outlaws wanted in the States was a gringo just begging to be robbed and murdered.

He felt no call to tell Clovinia along the way how he'd managed to make a few friends as well as a whole lot of enemies, just trying to do his job, on previous visits to Old Mexico. He knew some of it might sound like bragging. He knew she was only a messenger now. So he held off on the big question that was bothering him until she led the way up an alley, rapped softly on an oaken door set in a vast expanse of a dobe wall, and answered the challenge in the same Tsalagi lingo. It sure beat all how traditionally some folks acted as they got farther away from their old ways of life.

The male Cherokee who led them into the back patio through an arched passage was darker than Clovinia. Most everyone on Earth was, but he too could have passed for a plain old cowpoke if he'd had a mind to. He turned them loose in the patio to head back to the alley doorway with his own six-gun and ten-gauge Greener. So Longarm followed Clovinia on into a drawing room, where a considerable crowd had gathered at an ungodly hour as if to await the coming of the Lord, or leastways, somebody they were anxious to meet up with.

As Clovinia introduced him to everyone by name, he counted noses to tally nine men and three more women, which was not the way he'd have written the duty roster had anyone asked him to. For the ratio of four women to ten men seemed awkward.

From his own military experience, Longarm felt it best for men to ride through tough times with no women at all to worry about. He could see how modern Mexicans and old-time armies that spent years out in the field away from home might want to let men bring their women along, as complicated as that could make a baggage train or bivouac. But four gals riding an owl-hoot trail with ten men through that lonesome Sierra Madre Occidental meant six men were fixing to feel they'd been screwed, or in point of fact, not screwed. So those in charge likely felt strongly that rank had its privileges and fuck the enlisted men.

He noticed that the mixed bag of Cherokee, or Cherokee breeds, were all young and fit-looking but one, and in various sizes, shapes, and colors, with most looking at least sort of Indian. And as he'd noticed before while meeting Cherokee, their looks had nothing to do with how Indian they might act.

The one man over forty was a beefy, graying cuss with a firm handshake who was introduced as Reverend Gibson. It figured he'd prefer a white man's name. He looked more Cherokee than Chief Dennis Bushyhead up yonder in Tahlequah.

He said, "We've been anxious for you to join us, Deputy Long—or let's keep saying Tenkiller. Breakfast will be served in just a few minutes, and I'm afraid I don't hold with serving strong drink."

Longarm smiled and said, "I don't mind waiting for my grub, and I seldom drink anything stronger than coffee before noon."

Then he thought to ask uncertainly, "Uh, you do hold with coffee and tobacco, don't you, Rev?"

The older man said, "Certainly. We're Southern Baptists. We're not godless Mormons! Our Texas friends advise me it might be best if we crossed over into Mexico under cover of darkness. Have you anything to say about that?"

Longarm's smile grew more certain as he said, "I'm glad to hear you're willing to let me have some say. Crossing the river after sundown would be even safer if we crossed two by two at quarter-hour intervals to regather well south of the far shore, once we saw nobody seemed to be laying for us."

A younger Cherokee Longarm recalled being introduced as Jim Whitemark sounded unconvinced as he asked, "What if somebody *is* laying for us and only two of us ride into their ambush?"

Longarm made a mental note that Whitemark was likely old Gibson's *segundo* as he answered bleakly, "They'll be killed or captured. So that's why it's best to move in two by two. Old war stories are old bore stories. So suffice it to say, military commanders as far back as the Bronze Age found out, the hard way, it's best to risk losing one or two point riders than your whole outfit."

One of the gals, the brown-haired Miss Bluejacket, raised a hesitant hand to timidly ask, "Isn't there some safer and surer way to ride into uncertain surroundings, Mr. Tenkiller?"

Longarm shook his head and explained. "If there was, armies could save themselves a heap of bother and march into enemy territory without loading themselves down with guns and ammunition, ma'am. You look too young to have been there, no offense, but an otherwise fine military engineer named George McClellan snatched defeat from the jaws of his victory at Antietam by searching for a safe way to chase after Robert E. Lee once he'd licked him. I know it don't seem fair, ma'am. But if you're waiting for me to tell you how to invade Mexico during troubled times and ride close to four hundred miles down through the Sierra Madre Occidental without taking any chances at all, you may as well ask me how high is up or how long will eternity last. For I don't have answers to those questions neither."

Reverend Gibson chuckled knowingly and declared, "*Those* questions are *my* department, and I can see the grim logic to your suggestions on crossing the Rio Grande, ah, Mr. Tenkiller. Aside from cutting our losses in case of an ambush, two riders crossing the river at any one given time are less likely to be reported than a more suspicious column of fourteen riders leading another fourteen pack ponies, eh?"

Longarm shook his head and said, "I was about to get to that part. The Mexican authorities know you're here. They know you're Cherokee and they knew what you were up to before I did. I thought they might have things wrong when I heard they thought you'd come looking for those same lost, strayed, or stolen Cherokee George Guess had been looking for back in '43. But whether they know just where that cut-off mission might be or not, they're either for or against the notion of your expedition, so . . ."

"Who could have told them? How could they have told *you*?" the older leader of the expedition asked with a bushy-browed scowl.

To which Longarm could only reply, "I don't know who told them. But let me count the ways. Two can keep a secret if one of them is dead, and Lord only knows how many sneaks El Presidente Diaz has planted in our Land Management Office or even on your reservation. Having a love-hate relationship with Washington and Wall Street, Diaz needs to know, and pays well to know, what's going on north and south of the border."

Reverend Gibson sighed and said, "I see what you mean about keeping secrets. But who told *you*, and did they tell you whether they knew the location of our friends stranded in that mountain mission?"

Longarm didn't look Clovinia's way as he replied, "They sent two spies in a row to verify the rumor before I'd been in El Paso a full hour. So they knew I was coming. They may or may not have known who I really was. Odds are they'd have sent assassins instead of spies if they had me down as their wanted El Brazo Largo instead of good old Roger Tenkiller. The first spy they sent was clumsy. The second was more clever."

"Pretty too," said Clovinia Spotted Deer, as if butter wouldn't melt in her mouth.

Longarm smiled sheepishly and continued. "She was the one who said the friends I told her I was waiting for at the hotel were Cherokee, looking for the folks Sequoya, as she called George Guess, had been searching for back in '43. I didn't want her to know I knew she was a spy. I didn't think she knew what she was talking about. So we just never got into whether she knew the location of that mission or not."

"What *did* you get into then?" asked Clovinia with a Mona Lisa smile.

Longarm ignored her, saying, "The point is, they know."

Reverend Gibson sighed wearily and asked, "What do you suggest we do about that then? Would it help or hurt us if we simply went on over to the Mexican consulate here in El Paso and applied for visas?"

Longarm answered simply, "I don't know. If they said no and we crossed anyway, it might give them the excuse they were waiting for to smoke us up good. At the very least you'd be tied up here, north of the border, long enough for someone at the consulate to get around to asking Mexico City, by *mail,* and then long enough for somebody in Mexico City to write back. Let's be optimistic and settle on a figure of six to eight weeks."

There came a collective intake of worried gasps, and Gibson said, "Our endangered missionaries can't hold out that long."

Longarm started to ask how he could say how long anyone surrounded by uncertain numbers of friends or foes might or might not hold out. But he had to agree that if they were in any danger at all, six or eight weeks would be pushing their luck.

Reverend Gibson said, "We asked for you because we'd been told you know your way around down there better than anyone else our political allies could suggest. So what do you think we ought to do?"

Longarm declared, "If I was in total command I'd leave

the ladies and yourself here in El Paso, Reverend. Then I'd cull the rest of these boys as to how much rough riding they had under the seats of their pants, and then I'd head south with a five-man diamond or basic field patrol, traveling light, with extra guns and plenty of ammo. I'd figure on picking up food and water for the trip back once we got through to find those missionaries ready to ride back with us on ponies available down yonder. They'd have arms I'd issue them and such food and water as we could buy or commandeer from those friendly local Cherokee."

He hesistated, saw there was no nicer way to put it, and finished up with. "If they ain't still alive and well, amid friendly locals, they don't need to be rescued. So I'd do my best to get myself and my own diamond back alive, by way of another route. Unfriendly rabbit hunters are a caution when they catch you following the same trail the way a rabbit is inclined to."

All four women had started to bitch before Longarm had gotten that far. Reverend Gibson was saved from having to take a stand by a Mexican or full-blood maid coming in to declare breakfast was being served.

So old Gibson allowed he'd study on what Longarm had suggested, and they all trooped into an adjoining dining room to sit down in a bunch at a massive trestle table groaning under fourteen platters of *huevos rancheros,* stacks of tortillas, and coffee, tea, or hot chocolate in big earthen pitchers. Logarm felt so sleepy by this time that he'd forgotten he was hungry till he dug into the Tex-Mex breakfast provided by their unseen or absent white host.

Seeing that they couldn't leave until the end of a day just starting, no matter what they decided, Longarm elected to wash down his hearty grub with hot chocolate. When one of the Cherokee gals said she'd been sort of startled by Mexicans serving chocolate, hot or cold, Longarm almost told her that chocolate, or *chocolatl* as the Aztecs had called it, was a Mexican invention. But he was tired of talking about Mexico with greenhorns from the Indian Territory. He just washed down his *huevos rancheros* with chocolate, and didn't argue when one of the gals suggested that since they weren't going anywhere, it might not be a bad notion to catch up on as much rest as they could before they rode.

When he got up from the table declaring he hadn't caught much sleep the night before, another gal allowed she'd show him to one of the many guest rooms in the rambling pile. He excused himself for the time being and trailed after the helpful suggestion with his Yellowboy. Behind them, he heard Clovinia Spotted Deer stamp a high-button's heel on the tile floor as she whispered, "For heaven's sake, it's six o'clock in the morning and haven't either of you a lick of shame?"

# Chapter 8

"That poor lonesome squaw must want you bad," said the other gal he was trailing along a hallway, once they were out of earshot. That was something to study on. "Squaw" sounded odd as well as insulting coming from a Cherokee.

Eastern Algonquin called a lady a squaw, while western Cheyenne had decided the word was pronounced more like "esquaw." But other nations naturally used other words, and Cherokee, he was sure, called a woman something that sounded like *"Ah-gay-hew."* So naturally Indians with other words for womankind, hearing white men call the Indian whores of the tipi towns around their stockades "squaws," thought it a white man's word for a whore, and behaved accordingly whenever a white called his wife or mother a squaw.

The gal he was following looked more like an Indian than the blond Clovinia Spotted Deer, but then, so did *he* when you thought about it.

She'd been introduced to him as Miss Baker, and she'd asked him to call her Fran. The hair pinned up to expose the creamy nape of her neck was straight, shiny, and black as a raven's wing. He admired the rest of her rear view as he ambled along behind a flouncy Dolly Varden skirt and trim-waisted bodice of polka-dot calico. Black polka

58

dots on lemon yellow. He'd forgotten how pretty she was until she led him into an adobe-plastered guest room furnished Mexican-style, and turned to face him some more.

She had one of those heart-shaped little faces men tended to lose track of until they met up with them again and remembered how perfect they'd seemed all those other times. Her eyes were a sort of jarring blue for her sort of Latin features and jet black hair. Longarm had lost count of how many pretty little blue-eyed brunettes there were in the world with a sort of family resemblance. If there was anything to the notions of that Professor Darwin, some little old blue-eyed brunette had been popular as all get-out before the white race had spread far from its first hunting grounds.

She waved a hand expansively and said, "Make yourself at home and if there's anything you need, just pull that cord near the head of the bedstead and one of the household help will come a-running."

Then she took a deep breath, looked him straight in the eye, and asked, "If I *did* go to bed with you, would you change your mind about letting us girls play?"

Longarm managed a poker face—it wasn't easy—as he gravely replied, "I wouldn't change my mind for any price, Miss Fran. But the deciding ain't up to me. So you'd be wasting your kind offer on a no-good cuss who has no say as to who goes and who stays put."

She neither blushed nor looked away as she brazenly replied, "Oh, I don't imagine you'd be no good at all. We've heard a lot about you here in West Texas, Longarm. Didn't you have a sort of wild and woolly fling with that other big blonde who owns all that property over on the Gulf Coast?"

Longarm smiled thinly and said, "That's betwixt any such lady and me. There's some things a gentleman don't talk about and, no offense, you seem pretty free with your lip as well as our host's house and help."

She laughed lightly and explained, "I am your host.

Hostess leastways, whilst my daddy is away on other business. Did you think I was one of those fool Cherokee we're backing?"

To which he could only reply, "As a matter of fact, I did. I take it your daddy grazes a herd or more up on the Cherokee Outlet?"

She shook her head and said, "No, but a lot of my daddy's friends do. My daddy is with the El Paso party machine, and the name of the game in party politics is pleasing as many friends as you can make."

He didn't ask if she meant rich and powerful friends. He was paid to ask sensible questions, not stupid ones.

So he asked, "Does your daddy know you were planning to ride along with Reverend Gibson's rescue mission, Miss Fran?"

She shrugged and replied, "He isn't here. I wouldn't need his permission if he was. I'm free, white, and twenty-one. Or nineteen leastways, and somebody has to protect our family and party interests. How would it look if this handful of breeds rode off to nowhere with our blessings and a whole lot of money? We don't really know these folks. Friends in the Interior Department say Reverend Gibson is all right. But they don't have the blessings of the Cherokee tribal council. I'm not sure any Cherokee in position to get our money back knows a thing about this expedition, and what if it's just a confidence game?"

"What sort of a confidence game?" Longarm asked, even as he tried to come up with a sensible swindle.

She shrugged and replied, "How should I know? Confidence men don't tell you how they aim to cheat you. All I can say for certain is that we've sunk an awesome amount of political pull and financial backing into a rescue mission that hasn't gone far enough to matter. So what if Reverend Gibson and his bunch just ride a few miles into Old Mexico, turn around, and cross back farther west into, say, New Mexico Territory?"

"They're more likely to run into trouble as some mighty dry and empty country warms up with each passing day. That *would* make a swell stretch to sneak back into the States, if the Ninth Cav wasn't patrolling it right now. But assuming Reverend Gibson could charm his way past any border patrols he met up with, once he'd murdered me, that is, how much money are we talking about?"

She said, "I can't give you exact figures. They've spent a lot of it here in El Paso, just gearing up. But he did say he needed what he called a war chest of a thousand silver dollars."

Longarm nodded and explained, "Every outfit riding far through such uncertain surroundings needs a war chest or at least a money belt in case of unforeseen expenses in the field. General Washington was pleased as punch at Yorktown when he captured the literal chest full of money Cornwallis had been lugging all over Old Virginia. For unlike General Cornwallis, General Washington was expected to *pay* for the food and fodder it took to keep his Continental Army going."

He thought and decided, "If we leave you and me out, that leaves a thousand dollars to be split ten ways. Or a hundred dollars apiece. I know that's better than two month's pay for a top hand, but it's still slim pickings for members of a criminal conspiracy as drawn out and complicated as this one, if your notion is true. Don't forget, the whole bunch does hail from the Indian Territory, and none of them would ever be able to return to their kith and kin after the murder of a federal agent. So that would be asking a heap for no more than a hundred dollars."

She glanced out in the hall as if to make certain they were speaking in private before she asked, "Why would they have to be planning to kill you? What if they only mean to tie you up, and what if the three Cherokee girls were left out when they divided the pot. Outlaws don't have to share with their doxies, do they?"

Longarm's voice was certain as he gravely told her,

"They do if they have a lick of sense. Sporting Jenny in that Irish song wouldn't be the first nor the last outlaw gal to turn a road agent in for more money than she'd have wound up with being true to him. As for tying me up and leaving me behind just south of the border, I'd as soon be shot in the head and have it over with than lie there wondering if Apaches or *rurales* would stumble over me before I died of thirst and ant bites. I don't want to get into why they'd have to kill me either sudden or slow if they wanted to double-cross the party your daddy and my boss owe their patronage to. I was brought up not to brag."

Then he yawned in spite of himself before he could get his hand up to his face. Fran Baker smiled up at him and demurely remarked on his nice teeth, and suggested they talk about it some more later, when he was awake.

Once he'd shut the door after her, Longarm was surprised at how long it took him to wobble over to the bedstead, lean his Yellowboy against the adobe, hang his six-gun on a bedpost, and strip down. He turned in with his double derringer wedged between the mattress and the headboard. He fluffed the pillows, pulled the covers up over his head to shut out the morning light, and the next thing he knew he seemed to be tied to a stake with the blue-eyed brunette Fran Baker and the black-eyed blond Clovinia Spotted Deer dancing all around him, stark naked, save for those eagle-feathered warbonnets!

He murmured, "That's silly. One of you is only part Cherokee whilst the other's pure Texican. So where did you get them Cheyenne bragging feathers?"

Neither answered, and the next thing he knew he had to take a leak bad, but there was somebody locked in the Pullman crapper, and when he went out on the platform to let fly between cars, he found the Reverend Gibson there jawing with two Mexican nuns. So seeing he had to either wake up or piss in bed, he woke up.

Swinging his bare feet to the tile floor, Longarm bent

double to see if there was a chamber pot under the bed. There wasn't. He cussed and thought about yanking that pull-cord. Then he glanced at the dust motes dancing in the slanting afternoon sunlight through the window slats and had a better notion. He figured he could hold his water while he got dressed and hauled on his boots and gun rig. He left his hat and the Yellowboy to go out in search of a place to pee. His need was getting desperate by then, and he wondered as he wandered through the house whether he'd get caught if he pretended he was one of those white-wigged French courtiers at Versailles. He'd read how the imposing palace of King Louis the Fourteenth had sprawled out in a tangle of marble halls and fountained courtyards at awesome expense without anyone considering where anybody ought to crap. Hence the lingering odors tourists still noticed as they wandered through the palace of Versailles, wondering where *they* could take a crap or at least a leak. For generations, fancy-dressed nobility had pissed discreetly in secluded stairwells or taken a crap in window seats.

Longarm was saved from pissing in a hall corner when a Mexican porter came along, just in time, to tell him about the latrine just around the corner. He consulted his pocket watch as he drained his bladder with a sigh of relief, and saw it was just after five P.M. So most of that time in bed had been spent in dreamless sleep, and that was likely the reason he felt so much wider awake.

Buttoning up, he headed back to his guest room to fetch his hat and saddle gun. Turning a corner, he met up with Clovinia Spotted Deer. The Cherokee blonde said, "I just came from your room. Or the room Fran said you were in, that is. I see the two of you spent the day in *her* room instead?"

Longarm said in a firm but not downright nasty tone, "I can't say where Miss Fran spent the day. I spent it where she told you all she'd put me. Then I got up to take a piss out back. If you are interested in whether I

63

fuck women or not, I do, every chance I get, unless they say no or I don't like 'em. For I'm a natural man, bound by no wedding vows or other dumb promises to anybody. Are there any other questions?"

Her high-cheeked face glowed rosy red as she fought for composure and managed, "I suppose you're going to tell me you never messed with that Mexican girl back at the Eagle Hotel?"

Longarm hesitated, then decided, "Since she was a spy up to no good, I feel free to say she sucked me off as well. What are you aiming to do about that, file for a divorce, or report me to the principal?"

She gasped. "Oh, you're just horrid! Reverend Gibson sent poor me to fetch you again. He thinks we ought to share an early supper and mount up to ride as the sun is setting."

Longarm allowed he'd go get his hat and saddle gun if she cared to go on ahead. But she traipsed back to that guest room with him. He had no idea why. She'd just said they wanted him up front. So how come she seemed a tad disappointed when he just gathered up his Stetson and the Yellowboy and said, "Let's go"?

Later, having supper with Clovinia seated to his left and Fran Baker across the table from them, he listened politely without any comments of his own as the graying Reverend Gibson pontificated on his reasons for dragging the whole bunch, four women and all, over the river and into the chaparral, come what may.

Nobody had ordered Longarm to command the expedition, and since the old fart had made up his own narrow mind about that, Longarm was more concerned by the knowing glances he was getting from Fran Baker. The brown-haired Alice Bluejacket was staring dubiously down at her side dish of Mex frijoles, likely wondering what a pile of what could pass for dog shit might taste like. The most Indian-looking of the four gals, Margie McCash, was talking to or flirting with Jim Whitemark.

So Longarm figured the tingle he was feeling in his jeans had to be for the Cherokee blonde or the Texican brunette. But he wasn't all that certain he liked either of them that much. For as he'd sometimes confided to less experienced young gents, most any woman of most any description could kiss sweet as honey in the dark, but a man had to be careful lest he wind up with a beautiful bitch berating him to get a better job and start screwing her right. It wasn't true that a woman could castrate a real man with just her sharp tongue. But since parting could be such shrill sorrow, it was smarter to just never get started with a sharp-tongued gal, no matter how the rest of her was shaped.

You could see the Mexican kitchen help had been lectured on the Anglo notions of *chocolatl* when dessert was served in the form of a plain old chocolate and vanilla marble cake. Longarm's only suggestion was that everyone at the table should put away a couple of extra mugs of coffee. Since the Bakers were Texicans with pals in the cattle trade, the coffee was Arbuckle Brand, made strong. So Longarm took his neat, with no cream or sugar to dilute the caffeine. There was nothing he could do about it yet if anyone in the party fell asleep in their saddle by moonlight, being chased by Apaches, *los rurales,* or both.

# Chapter 9

After supper Longarm took old Gibson aside and suggested a couple of slight changes in their plans. Gibson agreed they might jump the border safer later if Longarm could drag a red herring across their trail back at the Eagle Hotel. He felt no call to tell a man of the cloth how he meant to slicker the Mexican secret service.

He wasn't even sure it would work, but it was worth a try and it figured to lull the tingle in his jeans leastways. He knew for dead certain that that Mexican maid at the Eagle was a two-faced sneak. But she sure kissed sweet, all over, with the pretty face she aimed at her victims.

So knowing she'd be on duty after sundown, Longarm went back with a fake request at the desk for any messages that might have come in for him, and then, since he'd never left officially, he wandered the halls until he saw Consuela had spotted him, and waited in his hired room until, sure enough, she came tapping on the door with a pitcher of ice water to ask where in thunder he'd been when she came back on duty hankering for more.

So he gave her more, knowing what she'd really come for as he came in her after pretending she'd been Clovinia Spotted Deer, Fran Baker, and what the hell, Miss Bluejacket and Margie McCash, as long as he was satisfying some urges.

Then he told her he couldn't stay long, and she said, "That's what *I* was about to say! Won't you be here when I get off duty, *querido mio*?"

He said, "Nope. You were right about them other Cherokee. They got in touch with me after you left last night. I've been over to the Baker town house with 'em most of the day."

He could tell from the way she accepted that without asking who in thunder the Bakers might be that he and Clovinia *had* been shadowed from the hotel the night before.

As they cuddled bare-ass atop the bedding he confided, "I don't know who told you. But you were on the money about them wanting to go visit Sequoya's grave for some fool reason. They asked me to show them the way because I've been south of the border as far as Ciudad Chihuahua. We'll be headed out later this evening. That's why I have to sign out downstairs and help them get ready."

She faked a yawn and asked in a desperately casual tone where they meant to cross the Rio Bravo, suggesting they might find it easier to just slip a few coins to the *rurales* on duty at the regular crossing, the way everyone else was supposed to.

He chuckled fondly and confided, "That's how I'd do it. But the old fuss in charge seems to think it's a secret that Sequoya died in Tamaulipas many a moon ago. I still don't know what they mean to do once I lead them to his grave. Seems a heap of bother if they're only fixing to put flowers on it. Mayhaps they mean to photograph it and sell prints to the folks back home. But my job is just to get them all there with wild Indians and worse raising Ned along the border. So I have to go along with the *big* Indian's orders, and we mean to cross the river northwest of El Paso, into New Mexico Territory."

She forgot to hide her sincere confusion as she asked,

"For why? Is *americano* on both sides of the Rio Bravo when you cross it in that direction, no?"

He said, "That's the point, if the old fuss *has* any sensible point. He fears . . . *ladrones,* as well as wild Indians, might be expecting a big party worth robbing to cross the river into Old Mexico. So he aims to cross where nobody would expect, then ride south through the higher country to the west, where our Hatchet Mountains cross an unmarked border to become your Sierra Madre Occidental, see?"

She replied sincerely, "No. Your leader must be *loco en la cabeza.* It's eighty miles west through Apacheria to the ranges of which you are speaking. After that, you would be riding through Nedli into Yaqui at a time both sides of the border are being patrolled by artillery as well as cavalry. I don't know about those Negro troopers on this side of the border. But *los federales* have orders to fire on distant moving dots with mountain artillery when they see such dots off the beaten tracks innocent ones are supposed for to follow! Would it not be simpler, and safer, if your friends just applied for visas and followed the regular *camino nacional*?"

He didn't ask an upstairs maid how she knew all that. He knew how she knew all that. So he just kissed her and had another quick piece before they parted friendly.

He went back to the Baker place, walking sort of funny, to assure the Reverend Gibson it might to be safe to cross the river downstream from the guarded ford, as they'd planned earlier.

He didn't go into the details of his ruse with a man of the cloth, but said, "They've doubtless got somebody watching this place. There's nothing we can do about that. But do we give them time to post scouts where I *told* them we'd be crossing the river, we can likely make our break for it downstream before the ones posted out front and back can get word to the Mex consulate about our change in plans."

68

The Reverend Gibson asked, "Won't that just be post-poning the inevitable? They'll know we're south of the border within hours, won't they?"

Longarm nodded and replied, "What were you expecting, egg in your beer? I told you right off they were expecting us to jump the border. They'd know where we'd headed if we had a tunnel running under the river from under this house, as soon as they noticed we weren't here anymore. I just went to . . . considerable effort to convince them we were headed into New Mexico upstream. Crossing downstream before they can shift any serious forces offers us a better chance. Not a sure bet, nor even an even chance. But better than no chance at all."

"What happens come the cold, gray dawn, with them knowing we're south of the border and having a good idea just where?" asked the older man.

Longarm said, "I told them we'd be headed for Tamaulipas, wherever that may be. Unless it's in just awful country I have in mind, they ought to expect us to be following a more sensible route, avoiding the quicksand washes and playas you have to cross to get to Yaqui country in the foothills of the Sierra Madre Occidental. It's Yaqui country to this day because neither armored conquistadors nor modern Mex artillery ever found it easy to move through the sort of soggy desert over that way. Naturally, it would make no sense for us to cross downstream instead of the way I told them, if we were really headed the way I told them we were headed."

"You gave away the route you mean to guide us along?" asked the Cherokee preacher with a confounded expression.

Longarm said, "I had to tell them we were aiming to head *some* fool direction, didn't I? The . . . Mex I mentioned the Sierra Madre route to allowed it sounded risky, doubtless because it is. Once they see I've led you another way, all wrong for riders making for the Sierra Madre Occidental, they ought to wire some wild wrong guesses ahead. They don't have enough riders here in El Paso to chase after us directly. Not with Victorio almost anywhere in the chaparral on either bank of the river. They'll wire *rurale* posts to the south to keep an eye peeled for us, hoping Victorio might save them all a heap of effort. Since we won't be headed the way I hope they'll think we're going, we shouldn't run into any *rurale* patrols."

The Reverend Gibson looked as if he might be having second thoughts as he asked, "What if we do? Worse yet, what if we run into Victorio and those Bronco Apache?"

To which Longarm dryly replied, "*Los rurales* might shoot on sight. They might keep an eye on us whilst they try to figure out our real game. I'm sure you have that hymn book with the advice that farther along we'll know more about it."

He let that sink in and added, "As to Victorio, I can tell you what him and his considerable band will do, but I can't seem to get you and the ladies to stay behind. My offer to take the point with a diamond patrol still stands."

The Cherokee preacher sighed and answered with another line of the hymn Longarm had cited. It went: "Cheer up, my brothers, walk in the sunshine. We'll understand it all, bye and bye."

So Longarm said, "Amen, if that's your final word. I'd like to see what we have to work with as to riding stock now."

So Longarm, the Reverend Gibson, and naturally their hostess, Fran Baker, went out back to the stable, a good-sized stable cum carriage house, where twenty-eight head, mostly of the Spanish Barb persuasion, were lined up with rumps facing rumps across a messy aisle. Longarm had no call to ask why they'd been keeping the trail stock hidden out of sight for a spell. But twenty-eight ponies dumped a lot of shit, and it was tough to talk in there without swallowing a buzzing stable fly.

Fran Baker's two Mexican stable hands had set aside their checkers when La Patrona and her guests had interrupted their game. After Longarm had finished a quick inspection, he told the three of them the ponies seemed in fair shape and suggested they get cracking with the riding and packsaddles from the tack room.

Getting fourteen bits and bridles, then fourteen *jaquimas* or rope hackamores in place was more than half the battle. All but one of the riding saddles already had saddlebags, saddle guns, and bedrolls in place. Longarm placed the saddle reserved for himself with empty saddlebags and gun boot aboard a bigger blue roan of, say, sixteen hands that could likely move sudden enough under a man his size. He told Fran Baker he'd tote his Yellowboy from the house when it came time to ride, and said he could pick up such possibles as clean socks and soap along the way. Then he explained how he'd traveled light down from Denver, and asked if she could spare him a tarp, a couple of flannel blankets, and maybe a rain slicker from her own possibles.

She said her help would make up a bedroll for him, and didn't look at the Cherokee preacher as she dryly murmured, "I'm sure you'll be bedding down on the trail alone, the first night or so."

Reverend Gibson didn't hear or decided not to show it. Protestants got to fire ministers who weren't good politicians. Calling down the wrath of Jehovah on sinners in general was one thing. Asking one of the whites backing your Indian cause to wash her mouth out with soap was another.

It was going on ten P.M. by the time they had everybody who was going along ready to go. The four gals had changed to more sensible split riding skirts and men's work shirts under sombreros or Texas gallons. They'd all been out in the Texas sun before Longarm had arrived.

Figuring the back alley was either being watched or it wasn't, they rode out of it in a bunch and followed a back lane east a couple of miles before they swung south across the bean fields of some folks Fran Baker knew, reining in amid the tangled alders and crackwillows along the Rio Grande.

Then, as per instruction, the rest of them waited while Longarm and young Jim Whitemark, who said he'd been a cowboy as well as an Indian on the Cherokee Reserve, tested the muddy waters of the rolling river. Fran Baker had allowed that the Rio Grande was shallow enough to ford without swimming your pony across that stretch. Longarm wondered what she considered deep by the time they were across, wet to their crotches.

But nobody seemed to be laying for them along a shallow stretch the local Mexicans had to know about as well. As they waited, Jim Whitemark asked Longarm what the Reverend Gibson had meant about sending him ahead with old Todd Scraper instead of Longarm himself.

Longarm softly replied, "I understand old Todd saw action at that battle of Pea Ridge, back when we were all more young and foolish. I forgot to tell him I rode in the war too. I disremember for which side."

The young breed, whose Indian blood showed more than old Gibson's, muttered, "I know why he wanted Scraper and me to ride on ahead. We all heard you tell him there was no surely safe way to take the point like we just did. That old Bible-thumping bastard was afraid you might get killed and we'd have nobody who knew Mexico as well as you to lead us!"

Longarm said soothingly, "He was doubtless thinking for the good of the greater number. The arithmetic is cruel, but logical. I knew the rest of you had been listening when I laid out the odds earlier. That's how come I took the point with you, against most of the rules of a ruthless science called military tactics. I say *most* of the rules because the only tactical move dumber than risking the loss of a leader would be to have all his followers think he'd rather risk *them*. Heaps of smart military leaders have gotten nowheres trying to push a floppy column ahead of them like a wet noodle. Dumber leaders such as

J. E. B. Stuart and George Armstrong Custer found they could lead a wet noodle most anywhere if they got out in front and just pulled it *after* them."

"Didn't both those great leaders wind up getting killed in battle?" asked the Indian cowboy.

Longarm nodded grimly and replied, "That's likely why some smarter West Pointers sent their men on ahead of 'em. But leading men into a fight the smart way is a contradiction in terms. You heard me suggest Reverend Gibson would be smarter to stay in El Paso and let me make a dumb try for them stranded missionaries. Taking the point with a fool like you was the next best tactic I could come up with."

Jim Whitemark's face was unreadable in the darkness under the trees along what was now the Rio Bravo. But his puzzlement was plain as he demanded, "How so? Even I can see, now that you've explained, how the rest of us would have to turn back if the only guide we have got his fool self killed or captured on us!"

Longarm quietly replied, "I just said that. There ain't enough of us to shoot it out with Victorio or even one troop of Mex *federales*. So by pulling instead of pushing a corporal's squad, an old man and four females, I just might be able to wriggle this expedition through to the headwaters of the Rio Verde. If I can't do it, none of you will be able to do it, and you'll be better off running for home."

Jim Whitemark suppressed a shudder and said, "Lord Jesus, you sure paint a rosy picture. I'm tempted to run for home right now!"

Then he peered off across the moonlit muddy water and added, "Aw, shit, it's too late now. Here comes Todd Scraper and Stretch Tiawa and, what the hell, the fucking greasers haven't killed us yet!"

To which Longarm couldn't resist replying, "Just give them time, old son. The night is young and none of us have made it a furlong south of that river yet."

# Chapter 10

Longarm had been unfamiliar with the river ford Fran Baker knew about. But he *was* familiar with the overall lay of the land, since he'd been chased back and forth across it more than once. So before midnight he had his bearings and had worked the group over to a bigger *camino de correos* or post road bound for Mexico City, if you followed the wagon ruts that far.

He explained to more than one Cherokee who asked that so close to the border as they still were, it would have been dumb to leave the beaten track and offer an easy trail to follow across the semiarid landscape of Northwest Chihuahua.

The country all about was considered *semi*arid because there were water holes and seasonal streams fed by the widespread islands in the sky that the Mexicans called *picos* if they stood alone, or *sierras* when they lined up as jagged-ass ridges, mostly running northwest to southeast. You couldn't see as far as any high country in the darkness all around, of course. So Longarm felt no call to lecture his charges from the Indian Territory on the dramatic changes in temperature and humidity a rider met up with in this particular desert.

Longarm had long since learned, having come west just

after the war from the hills of West-by-God-Virginia, how that one word, "desert," covered mighty varied scenery, from the downright green cactus forests of the Sonora to the no-shit white sand dunes east of the Jornado de Muerto or the poisonous depths of the aptly named Death Valley.

Some Cherokee still dwelt in their old home range in what were now the green hills of Tennessee. Old Andy Jackson's roundup had been a brutal but careless affair, and how was a cavalry trooper from other parts supposed to know or really give a hang when some ragged-ass hill folks lazing on their cabin's steps insisted they were Scotch-Irish as pure as the driven snow, God damn your eyes.

The western or official Cherokee still liked to bitch about that "Trail of Tears," more like "The Trail Along Which We Cried," if anyone cared to use the Tsulagi name, and it was true the Indian lands set aside west of the Big Muddy got less rain than Tennessee. But they got better than twenty inches a year, and the Cherokee Allotment bordered by Kansas to the north and Arkansas to the east had been a patchwork of hardwood forest and tall-grass prairie the last time Longarm had looked. So while there was no doubt that all five of the Civilized Tribes had been handed the short end of the stick, they were laying it on a mite thick when they pissed and moaned about having been driven into the "Great American Desert" to starve.

Folks with as much or more Indian blood managed to keep from starving in this far-drier Chihuahua Desert. From time to time as they rode on through the night, they'd spy distant pinpoints of candlelight to show where some Mexican family was making out, poor or prosperous, depending on how they sat with the current government.

The Chihuaha got rain all year on widely scattered and often wild occasions. It got more sunlight than even Jack's beanstalk needed to grow, provided it got irrigated good. So the local Mexicans were skilled as all hell when it came to irrigation, and you'd see fields of corn higher than Don Quixote on horseback, with squash big enough to serve as Cinderella's coach, surrounded by square miles of dusty birdcage gravel, where sticker brush and prickly pear toughed things out as they waited for rain under a tediously clear sky.

At about two in the morning, Longarm, in the lead, spotted more than one point of light dead ahead. He reined in to study on their next best move. When the Reverend Gibson and Stretch Tiawa joined him, Longarm explained, "Wide spot in the road ahead. Likely a stage stop, with a telegraph office. Starting to quiet down for the night."

Stretch Tiawa said, "It's way after midnight! What would a village of lazy Mexicans be doing up at this hour?"

Longarm replied, "Same thing we're doing. Moving about when such moving's less sweaty. They ain't that lazy all the time. Just when it's too hot to work, during La Siesta from, say, noon to four in the afternoon. The bunch ahead will turn in for a few hours, now that it's a tad too *cold* for bare feet and cotton duds. Then things will start to hum again until noon."

He heeled his mount forward at a walk. When they wanted to know why, he explained, "We want 'em to notice us as we pass through, headed for Sequoya's grave, I reckon."

The Cherokee preacher blinked in surprise and demanded, "Won't that give away our secret border crossing? I understand the telegraph lines are owned by the government down here and—"

"I just now said I *wanted* them to report our passing through in a logical direction," Longarm explained. "There's no way *los rurales* won't be told where we crossed the river, if they haven't already been told. They surely had somebody watching the Baker place back there in El Paso. I thought I'd explained how I only hoped to befuddle them a tad in hopes of getting a *lead* on them. As we ride in, I want you gents to hang back at staggered intervals. Should I sense a trap, I'll either signal or go down trying. In either event, you gents will have to get everyone back across the border as best you can and inform your backers I was right about this being too big a boo at this time!"

Then he rode on alone before anyone could argue. Dogs in any breed of village always seemed to pick a stranger out at a distance. So more than one human villager was staring thoughtfully as Longarm rode along the center of the *camino* into town, Yellowboy across his thighs and eyes peeled for any sign of a *rurale* station.

*Los rurales,* like the Canadian Mounties El Presidente had stolen the notion from, patrolled the rural highways and byways between towns, and left policing the towns themselves to local *alcaldes* and such town law as they fancied. But like the Mounties, and of course like the Texas Rangers who'd been first with the notion west of the Big Muddy, all such roving mounted police were headquartered in some town or the other along the rural roads they policed.

As luck would have it, there seemed to be no *rurale* post in what turned out, in fact, to be a stage depot, a church, a telegraph office, and a cantina wrapped around a small market square. The stalls out in the square had been put to bed for the night under straw matting. A lamp gleamed in the telegraph office. The church and stage depot were dark, and he saw no stock in the pole corral where you'd expect to spy fresh teams.

They'd know at the cantina—and cantinas stayed open until there was no hope of any regular knocking off from his own chores dropping by on his way home.

Longarm could tell from the barking behind him that his Cherokee pals had decided he might live and were coming in to join him. So Longarm reined in, dismounted, and tethered his own mount as he waited there for the preacher and old Todd to ride within earshot. He called out, "Rev, you'd best ride back and tell the others to hold up until I send Todd out to you. Seeing as I can't hardly do that unless you're at hand, Todd, what say I buy you a drink inside?"

The Indian cowboy didn't have to have his arm twisted. So it wasn't long before the two of them were bellied up to the bar inside, nursing clay mugs of pulque as the fat and friendly Mexican behind the bar brought them up to date on that deserted stage depot across the way. The one word "Apache" would have sufficed, but the local kept explaining how much Apache liked to dine on stagecoach mules. The two Americans sipped warm pulque, and Todd Scraper murmured in English, "What's this puke we're drinking? It tastes the way I've always imagined the contents of a cuspidor might!"

Longarm said, "I doubt anybody's really spit tobacco juice in it. Pulque is to tequila as beer is to bourbon. Same ferment before they run it through the still. The best pulque, like real tequila, is made from *maguey*, a Mex sort of agave or century plant. But they use other agaves and even cactus pads if you don't watch 'em. Why don't you go fetch the others in, Todd? They could all use a set-down, and I'll ask if these folks can fix us up with some tamales and such to remember on the trail whilst we dine on cold, canned grub."

Todd Scraper allowed he'd rather do anything than finish a whole mug of snail slime. So the cantina was soon filled to overflowing as both the Cherokee rescue mission and a heap of curious villagers crowded in for late snacks and a nightcap. None of the Cherokee liked pulque all that much. But the Texican gal, Fran Baker, allowed she'd had some of the awful stuff before, and seemed game enough to try more.

Or so she'd said, before Longarm noticed how she

seemed to be using their belly-up as an excuse to low-rate the other gals in the bunch.

Longarm would have agreed with her notion that the three Cherokee gals were useless baggage if it hadn't been coming from *her*. He tried to change the subject politely. But when Fran got to ranting about the repeating rifle and two six-guns packed by the brown-haired Alice Blue-jacket, Longarm snorted in disgust and said, "Make up your mind. Neither you nor me has any say-so in the matter. So the gals are riding with us whether we like it or not, and would you rather ride with some shrinking violet who can't look after herself or a country gal packing plenty of hardware?"

He couldn't resist asking her innocently, "Can I count on you to back my play with your own repeating rifle and six-guns when and if such dramatics may be called for, Miss Fran?"

She blazed, "You know full well I've a seven-shot Spencer .52 in my saddle boot, and my daddy's taught me how to use it too! As for side arms, I've a Webley .455 Bulldog in my bedroll if I should ever need to defend myself with a pistol."

Longarm dryly remarked, "I'd unpack it and carry it handier then. When you need a pistol you need one bad, and you may not have time to unroll your bedding. Or do you argue a lot in bed too, ma'am?"

She stamped a foot and moved off through the crowd with her drink. That gave Longarm the chance for a few words in private with some of the other men.

Within the hour the Reverend Gibson had announced it was time to move out. Longarm assured them they'd come to a larger village with shade and more refreshments before the sun rose high enough to matter.

The locals watched, laughed, flirted, and even helped as the party saddled up and got on its way again.

The Mexican secret service agent in peon costume who'd trailed the rescue mission all the way from the

Baker place in El Paso waited to give them enough time to be well on their way before he slipped over to the telegraph office. The clerk on duty had turned in for the night, and said so loudly when he finally responded to some serious pounding on his side door.

The secret agent he'd taken for an unshaven drunk flashed a badge and told him to do a really dreadful thing to his mother, then warned him what dreadful things they would do to certain lazy *cabrónes* who refused to send urgent messages. The telegrapher let him in and asked him who and what he wanted to wire.

The sneak who'd tailed Longarm and his pals thus far wired El Paso a progress report, putting the *gringos chingados* on the post road to Ciudad Mejico. Then he wired ahead to advise *los rurales* they were coming. Or he tried to. The government telegraph operator looked up from his telegraph set to sigh and explain, "The line is dead to the south. Has been no high wind. Could be Victorio?"

The secret service man in ragged white cotton muttered about that *diablo chingado,* and told the telegrapher to wire north if he could. He didn't have to issue further instructions. A telegraph operator who didn't know how to phrase it when Bronco Apache took to cutting telegraph lines was by definition hardly a telegraph operator!

The agent left to stride over to the *alcalde*'s office cum residence, where another heated exchange took place. When you "woke up" a Mexican official who'd just gone to bed, you seldom found him in bed alone. But once they'd pulled rank back and forth and got that out of the way, the *alcalde* allowed he could fix the secret service up with a posse soon enough.

The agent in ragged cotton explained he only needed a few good men to back his play, should he run into *others* along the way. He said, "Someone has cut the telegraph line south to the next outpost. We live in troubled times. So could be troublemakers a few good government men could handle if they are still around out there in the dark."

The *alcalde* soberly asked, "What if the line was cut by *los indios*? Those Apache we were warned about, or *Dios mio*—Yaqui no Christian *has* to be warned about?"

The secret service man shrugged and replied, "My orders were for to keep an eye on those mysterious Christian Indians who entered our land illegally tonight. Was nothing said about fighting *other* Indians. But we have talked about thes matters enough. I wish for to ride. So where are those other *chingado* riders, eh?"

You didn't stay *alcalde* of even a small village by arguing with an agent of the current dictatorship. So within minutes the sneak from El Paso was riding south after the party Longarm had been ordered to lead. The agent and his riders were less than three miles south of the village when they heard the blood-chilling Apache war cry *"Dikah! Dikah! Heyheyheyhey!"* and one of them lost his hat to a shot from the dark!

They whirled their mounts to head the other way *muy pronto*, as what seemed like a dozen rifles from the roadside chaparral sped them on their way screaming about an Apache ambush.

Even the greenest hands among them could see what the villain Victorio had planned in advance with his usual cunning. Having cut the wire, the murderous Apache had set up an ambush for any repair crew!

But they'd fought their way free with the divine help of *Jesus, Maria, y Jose,* and they were still yelling about it as they rode out of earshot.

"That'll learn you!" said U.S. Deputy Marshal Custis Long of the Denver District Court, or El Brazo Largo, depending on which side of the border one asked, as he stood waist-deep in chaparral, reloading the tube of his Winchester Yellowboy.

For Victorio had had nothing to do with cutting that wire, and, the man who'd cut it sincerely hoped, was off raising his own hell in other parts. But with any luck,

Longarm's simple ruse had bought them a little more time, and when you got right down to it, that was all one could hope to do with time. Buy as much as you could, any way you could, a little at a time.

# Chapter 11

Having told his charges where to wait for him, Longarm legged it to the blue roan he'd hidden in a prickly pear patch to ride after them. They didn't have that great a lead on him, thanks to that sneak he'd had a hunch about being anxious to catch up. So Longarm, the big blue roan, and the sunrise overtook the Cherokee rescue mission within sight of but still outside the next wide spot in the post road.

This time he had most of them wait in the cool, crisp morning light in the almost chilly shade of a roadside corn milpa. That sounded a tad sillier than it looked, a milpa being a raised irrigated corn patch and the corn growing tall under irrigation and the Chihuahua sun. Since Cherokee grew corn their own way, he had to explain to a couple of them that the Mexicans hadn't gone to that extra work just to show off. Irrigated cropland in desert country got too salty for crops in no time unless you made damned sure of the drainage. When you ran sunbaked ditch water over a plant's roots, you wanted it to just keep running off with its dissolved minerals after wetting the roots just enough. You didn't want all that calcite and sodium chloride, or plain old table salt, left behind as standing water evaporated in place, year after year.

Longarm had asked at the last village, but he still moseyed in ahead to make certain they'd been right about things being slow, due to that Indian scare.

Once he'd scouted the town and found it as safe a place to hole up for the day as he'd hoped, Longarm had his Cherokee charges bed down for the day where they and, above all, their riding and pack stock would be out of the Chihuahua sun, under the tile roofing of the big *posada* or under the rustic sun-silvered pole roofing of the *ramada* along one side of the municipal corral.

Longarm bedded down alone. It happened sometimes. He caught up on some needed sleep, treated himself to a set-down tub bath and a lazy man's shave at the *barberia,* and was just rising to leave when a sweaty cuss wearing a gray bolero jacket with matching sombrero came stomping in to announce, *"Este condenado calo me va a matar!"*

Then the *rurale* sergeant locked eyes with Longarm and added in thickly accented English, "What the fuck ju looking at, gringo?"

Longarm calmly replied in Spanish, "When a man speaks, is polite for other to pay attention, no? We were just speaking of how hot it is outside this afternoon, and one takes it you and your followers have ridden far?"

The burly Mexican semmed more mollified as he growled, "Far enough. I see you recognize me as a troop leader, eh? Not bad for a superior being from El Norte. Did I ever tell you about the gringo who mistook me in this uniform for that of a *cochero* and demanded to be driven to the *estacion ferrocarril*?"

Longarm smiled thinly and replied, "I wish I'd been there. Do you mind if I make a suggestion, *mi sargento*?"

The sweaty *rurale* regarded him with suspicion but told him to speak.

Longarm explained how he'd just treated himself to a tub bath in the back and how much cleaner and cooler he'd felt before sitting down for that shave.

The *rurale* considered, nodded, and decided, "Is not a bad idea, and if it works I will buy you a drink at the cantina once I am done here. How are you called and where shall you be found the next time I wish for to gaze into those big blue eyes, eh?"

Longarm laughed easily and said, "I am called Crawford. Sam Crawford. I was about to leave the *posada* now that it's started to cool off. I've been down in Durango on business. I'd like to get back to Texas *muy pronto* if half the things they say about Victorio are true!"

The sergeant said, "I will tell you what you should like, Crawford. Wait for me at the cantina. Later, after sundown, you will ride north with us for to feel safer, eh?"

So Longarm allowed they had a deal, and lit out before he had to tell more lies. He got to question liars a lot, and knew a liar had to have a good memory, or tell easy lies to remember. So that was why a man who rode for Uncle Sam decided to be a Sam, while Crawford worked as both the handle of a namesake, Dr. Crawford Long, the pioneer of painless surgery, and of Reporter Crawford, that pest who kept writing about Longarm in the *Denver Post*.

Knowing from his own experience how much one could keep track of in a big copper tub surrounded by tiles walls, Longarm got back to the *posada* on the double. A few desperately casual questions established that the sergeant he'd left soaking across the way was riding with no more than a dozen others. Since none were in sight outside at the moment, it seemed safe to assume they too had found other pleasures to indulge in after a hard ride along a lonesome road during an Indian scare.

Gathering the Cherokee preacher and some of the older men in private, Longarm explained the dumb bind he was in with *los rurales*. Then he asked if anyone there could navigate across open range by the stars once the sun had set. When the fussing simmered down, Longarm grinned and told them, "I had to ask and don't be so smug. Your

Pawnee cousins know the stars better than they really need to. My point in asking is that I'll never be able to catch up again this time unless I know the exact bearing you're following across the open desert to the west, see?"

They did, and seemed to have no trouble grasping his simple but vital order to ride west, due west, with no deviation from a beeline he'd be able to follow in the dark with the help of the same fool stars.

Then he said, "Let's get everybody mounted sudden to ride out slow in dribs and drabs, and meet up again out of sight from this village. Once you do, put as much distance as you can bewixt hither and yon. I might or might not be able to misdirect them *rurales*."

He was, of course. He waited at the cantina as the others snuck out of town. That burly sergeant joined him as some of his other pals were still leaving. But the big Mexican felt so much better, he allowed it was a shame they weren't both queer so he could kiss his new gringo pal.

Longarm could only hope the burly Mexican was joshing. He knew his eyes were more gun-muzzle gray than big blue, and he didn't feel half as pretty as his new *rurale* pal kept implying. Then there were the sly remarks about the both of them feeling so squeaky clean, now that they'd shared the same tub, if not at the same time, alas.

But as the shadows lengthened and the time grew nearer for all good *rurales* to saddle up and ride, Longarm decided that since none of his graceful exit lines seemed to work, there might be another way. So he ordered tequila for the both of them, and saw to it that his burly but uncomfortably friendly drinking partner somehow managed to drink for the two of them from both glasses.

That wasn't as tough as it sounded, once the sergeant had downed his first couple of hundred-proof tequilas. But if the liquor was clouding the man's judgment as a lawman on patrol for suspicious strangers, the personality changes were becoming downright scary.

Longarm read more than other working-class gents his

age. Reading wasn't quite as much fun as women, or even penny-ante poker. But as one drew closer to payday, reading was at least affordable, and so he'd read how gents who brushed their teeth with steel files and beat up sissy boys a lot were inclined to have secret longings they could only allow themselves to think about when they were drunk as skunks, or pretending to be. Longarm had known before he ever read it that many a mean drunk or silly drunk had more control of his feelings than he let on, even to himself. The light-headed feelings and sudden shifts of balance just made it way easier to take a swing at somebody you just didn't cotton to, drunk or sober, or grab the ass of someone you did. So Longarm wasn't surprised when his newfound friend suddenly blurted out in English, lest a couple of other *rurales* in the *cantina* doubt his manhood, "Hey, gringo. Ju like for to suck cock?"

Longarm managed to hold on to his poker face, although this wasn't easy, as he calmly replied, "Mayhaps. What will you do for me if I do that for you?"

The burly Mexican didn't remember how you offered to go sixty-nine in English, and knew his troopers would wonder if he suggested it in Spanish. So he suggested they just go upstairs to Longarm's room and see what the two of them might work out.

Longarm suspected the lower-ranking *rurales* knew more than their burly leader thought they knew about his personal life. One nudged a pal and murmured, *"Sin embargo, puede ser que la fantasia es mejor que le vera chupardera."*

Longarm was tempted to tell the softly smiling *rurale* what he could do with his own dirty daydreams, but it was smarter to let folks think you didn't know what they were saying about you when you didn't have time to fight them. So he just led their leader upstairs to his hired room and knocked him out in the dark, then caught the unconscious sergeant before he could thud to the floorboards. He placed the burly Mexican on the bedstead and shut the door before, working in the dark, he unbuckled the gun-belt, then the inner belt, to haul the victim's riding pants down around his booted ankles.

Then he hung the gunbelt and big sombrero neatly to leave a thumbnail impression of a satisfied but dead-drunk sodomist, should anyone risk peeking for the next hour or more.

He didn't care what the sergeant remembered once he came to again. The odds were against him remembering much. When a suspect told you the last thing he remembered was getting knocked out, you knew he was lying to you. A concussion tended to wipe out ten minutes or more leading up to the knockout blow.

Once he found out he hadn't been robbed, the *rurale* might think he'd had a lover's quarrel he just didn't want them to hear about at headquarters. It was more important that he wasn't likely to come to for at least another half hour or so, and better yet, it was dark out now.

So Longarm slipped down the back stairs and out to the corral to saddle his two ponies and lead them out of town at a walk before he mounted up and rode, not after his pals just yet, but further south to buy some more precious time.

Back at his furnished digs in Denver, Longarm had an army field telegraph key among his possibles. That was small help to him this far south, but there was more than one way to skin a cat or send telegraph messages. So he reined in to tether his mount to the base of a pole, then shinny up to where four wires were strung side by side to show it was a main line. Propping his elbows over the crossbar, Longarm opened a particular blade of his pocket knife, reworked by a locksmith who swore he only did that sort of thing for lawmen, and proceeded to saw through one of the wires.

He knew it didn't really matter which he chose. All Mexican telegraph lines led to Mexico City, the way all Roman roads had led to Rome. Once he had the wire severed, he'd naturally cut off the carrying current. So each time he touched the severed ends back together he clicked the receiving keys wherever they were hooked in. Late Victorian telegraph technology worked two basic ways. Fed by acid cells, the wires carried a constant current broken into dots and dashes by being switched off and on, or calling for more power, by bursts of current released along the line by on and off switches. Hanging by his elbows up a telegraph pole, Longarm could only thank the national grid for providing him with the carrying current he needed as, breaking and restoring the current with a wire end in each hand, he proceeded to send a message.

It wasn't easy trying for Spanish he wasn't fluent in, in Morse without a telegraph key. But what the hell, he was *trying* to *confuse* everybody. So he sent a garbled message warning everyone Victorio and his bunch had been joined by Mexican Nedli Apache. Then, having no tools to re-splice the wire, and having no call to resplice the wire, he let both ends of the fool wire fall and, as long as he was up there, cut the other three wires as well before he shimmied back down the splintery pole, laughing to himself.

Once down, he rode west by the stars, knowing he was beelining a few miles south of the main party but not trying to catty-corner up to any trail he couldn't see. It was better to know you were south of somebody for certain, than to overshoot or undershoot in the dark and have no idea *where* the hell they'd been when you figured you'd drawn even with them.

There was no trail at all, but the desert stretched flat in the moonlight, once the moon had risen in the east enough to matter, with the scattered clumps of low chaparral and taller cactus easy to avoid. He was making good time. Better time, he was certain, than the main party would be doing, for like a convoy of Spanish galleons back in pirate times, a larger party could move no faster than its slowest element, and thanks to restocking at those last two trail towns, some of those pack ponies would be moving mighty slow for the next few days on the trail.

So Longarm was alone in the middle of nowhere for a spell, and it was just as well he'd reined in to swap saddles when he heard distant, trotting hooves and muffled voices. Because that gave him the chance to lead his own stock into a thicket of paloverde and just lie low as the night riders approached, laughing and carrying on as if they'd been a bunch of young hands returning from a ride to town. Until they got a tad closer and he could make out some words being tossed back and forth at an uncomfortable but mile-eating trot.

Longarm didn't understand the words, of course. It was said you had to be raised Na-déné to grasp the most complicated Indian dialects of all. Some said they'd earned their Pima name "Apache," or "Enemy," just by being so infernally tough to understand. So a really lonesome white man wasn't about to say a word to them as they trotted past, chatting pleasantly about wine, women, and song, or maybe blood, guts, and torture, until they'd ridden on to wherever in thunder they'd been headed.

"That'll learn you fool Mexicans to call me names and post bounties on a poor wayfaring stranger!" he chortled as he finished his chores and rode on, leaving Mexico to worry about its other problems with strange riders.

It took him until well into the wee small hours to catch up with the main party, and it might not have happened at all had not he spotted the flash of a Cherokee lighting his pipe from a good three miles away. But Longarm still gave young Jeff Garner holy hell for striking that match without cupping the flame, and once the others heard about those Indians out in the dark, some of them gave the kid hell too.

# Chapter 12

The sunrise caught them strung out in stirrup-high chaparral with higher ground to the south overlooking the narrow trail Longarm had chosen. He proved he'd chosen well when he led them to a dry wash choked with mesquite rising high as crab apple trees and called a halt, reminding them not to build a fire. He pointed to the rocky crags to the south, declaring, "Yonder rises what the Mexicans call the Candelaria Hills. If I wasn't Victorio holed up in them, I'd as likely be Mex mountain artillery hunting for him. I rid through the maze with Mex pals on a previous occasion. That's how I know you can see forever out across these flats we're on right now. So leave us not send any woodsmoke up to get in the eyes of anybody perched atop any lookout rocks over yonder."

As he dismounted in the dappled shade to tether his blue roan to a tasty screw-pod mesquite in bloom, Reverend Gilmore and some other Cherokee joined him, muttering amongst themselves in Tsalagi. From their conversation, Longarm knew Gibson, young Jeff Garner, and old Todd Scraper had to be from the same Cherokee band.

The nominal leader of the rescue mission said, "We've been wondering why you've led us across these more exposed desert flats if you know a route through those canyon lands to the south."

Longarm said, "I thought I just told you. The Candelarias are just swell for hiding out in. One man with a rifle could hold off an army in some of the narrower passes. Them renegade Indians know that. So do the Mexican riders out to settle their hash."

"But what makes you suspect either Apache or Mexican troopers are over that way right now? Wouldn't we be safer hiding out among those crags than out here in the open, if nobody's there at all?"

Longarm snorted. "Well, sure we would. But if there's nobody else over this way, it hardly matters where we day-camp. Contrariwise, it *hurts* to get blown out of your saddle by a drygulcher who got there ahead of you. So I try to avoid swell hideouts and likely ambushes as I wend my weary way through hostile territory. That's what you call uncertain range where you might meet up with anybody. I told everybody back at the Baker place to fill at least one canteen with strong black coffee to be diluted and sweetened to taste down this way. But it might be best to just break fast on some cold, canned grub and catch some sleep this side of sundown, and save coffee for the night ahead."

The Reverend Gibson allowed he'd relay the advice. Longarm, not wanting to seem bossy, took his borrowed bedroll and used carbine up the south side of the wash to bed down amid the lower chaparral on the rim, where a man resting prone with a Yellowboy could keep a casual eye on those distant rimrocks just by raising his head from time to time.

Once he'd spread the groundcloth and flannel bedding, he improvised a patch of shade over the nest he'd fashioned between clumps of sticker brush. As he was doing so, a familiar feminine voice from behind him murmured, "Why do you people always call Indians *renegades*? A renegade is a traitor who's broken his word, isn't he?"

Longarm placed his Yellowboy in the meager shade he'd improvised and turned to tell the Cherokee blonde, Clovinia Spotted Deer, "Not hardly. A traitor is a cuss who's betrayed his own side. A renegade is a cuss who's betrayed his own word of honor. So lots of Indians, most Indians as a matter of fact, could hardly be called renegades, and so they ain't. Tashunka Witko—we called him Crazy Horse—led the charge at Little Big Horn with honor as a *hostile*, not no *renegade*, because he'd never surrendered and signed up for an allotment number with the Bureau of Indian Affairs. Victorio is a renegade because he did. He fought us under Cochise, and agreed to the peace Cochise made with us in '71. Then he broke his bond and riz again and again, until the army licked him fair and square in '77 and he agreed to accept six hundred square miles of New Mexico Territory as a reservation if he'd promise to behave."

Noting the blonde's Cherokee preacher didn't seem to be watching, Longarm fished out a cheroot and held it up for her to nod yes or shake her head no to as he went on. "Leave us not forget Victorio had been on a seventeen-year rampage and many a white man has been hanged for killing just one or two folks. I'll allow the B.I.A. could be said to have broken its bond with Victorio when it asked him to relocate to the San Carlos Reserve. But he could have said no, or even ridden off in a snit, without killing anybody. But Victorio and his band have been torturing and killing men, women, and children, Anglo, Mex, and other Indians, on both sides of the border with considerable glee. So that makes them renegades to me and most everyone else with a lick of sense."

She'd nodded, so he lit the cheroot and broke the match stem to be sure it was out as he dryly added, "I never meant to imply Cherokee were renegade Indians exactly. Having sided with the Confederacy and lost fair and square, you took your lumps in the Reconstruction, and since President Hayes has agreed to forgive and forget *that* fight, I reckon you're just plain Indians. Sort of. Would you care for a smoke of your own?"

The Cherokee blonde blinked in dismay and said, "In public, like a certain class of white girl? Certainly not, but thank you just the same. Why have you spread your bedding up here in the sunlight? It's much cooler down in this shady draw. Are you worried about a flash flood?"

Longarm exhaled and said, "You always worry about that in a desert dry wash. You worry about hostiles more, and you figure the odds on waking up underwater or under a stranger with his gun up your nose before you go to sleep. I sleep light with a worried mind and, perched up here, I may notice anybody headed this way a long time before they can get here. I called this halt because of the dust all our ponies were kicking up. I doubt either Victorio or *los federales* will venture out across these flats by daylight without good reason. They know about rising dust as well as we do. So why don't you get back under them trees and catch some sleep whilst I worry about uninvited visitors?"

She stayed put. It would have been rude to duck under that shady tarp with her still standing there in the morning sun. The sun was commencing to press warmer on the back of his shirt as it rose ever higher. It would have been forward to ask her what in thunder she wanted now. So he just waited until she asked why he hadn't assigned guard duty in rotation to the other men in the party.

He said, "It ain't for me to assign anything, ma'am. I was only sent down here unofficially to guide you all to that mission that ain't on any map. If I thought there was a serious chance of anyone else even starting out for the worse country ahead under that rising sun, I'd chance throwing some weight around early. But I have found it best to let strangers see you know what you're talking about before you start giving them orders. Lord knows, I may have to issue some odd-sounding orders a day or so down the trail ahead."

94

She asked what lay down the trail ahead, and he explained why few if any others would be pestering them on the flats further west. He told her, "Come this time tomorrow, Lord willing and we ain't been killed, we're going to have to reverse our hours of locomotion. It would be pure suicide to ride across the dead center of this basin in the dark, and we're unlikely to meet up with anybody, at any hour, as we thread our way southwest through mighty wide and uncertainly mapped seasonal lakes, swamps, or alkali flats, weather permitting. This faint burro trail we've been following so far likely runs off to a *federale* outpost at El Barreal on the north shore of a mighty big lagoon when there's water in it. We want to swing north of El Barreal under cover of darkness. Then we're going to have to risk a daylight dash to the south along a sometime desert stream they call the Santa Maria. Mexicans are short on original place names. If we can get around the dry sink or lagoon of the Santa Maria, we'll have her quicksand streambed betwixt us and any Mexican Christians. We'll have pagan Yaqui not too far off to our west, but they may not be scouting that far east, and at the least Yaqui don't drag mountain howitzers after them."

"Are you trying to frighten me?" Clovinia demanded. "If you are, you're doing a pretty good job. I can see why those missionaries need to be rescued as I never saw before! Do you think they're in any danger from those . . . Yaquis?"

Longarm said, "Not until we try to bring them back through Yaqui country. The Yaqui claim to be unreconstructed Aztecs who never gave up their fight with His Most Catholic Majesty or anybody trying to run Mexico since. They're as tough and mean as you'd expect Aztec holdouts to act. But they only occupy a mountain stronghold about the size of your Indian Territory, along the Continental Divide south of the New Mexico line. I've rid through Yaqui before. I've fought them on occasion, and even made common cause with them on occasion. They hate Mexican troopers and lawmen more than they hate anybody, and they hate most everybody a lot. So, all in all, I mean to avoid both the Yaqui and the Nedli, the Mexican versions of Apache. Some say Victorio, or at least his momma, was Nedli Apache, or Na-déné as they call themselves. I'm sure starting to feel that sun on my back, ma'am. I don't suppose you'd care to join me under the shade of that tented tarp?"

It worked. She told him he was just horrid and ran back down among the sheltering mesquites.

So he peeled off his sweaty shirt as long as he was about it, and slid headfirst into his outpost to discover that, as he'd hoped, it was way cooler in the shade atop chaparral-sheltered earth that only got a few hours of direct sunlight around noon.

He set his Stetson aside as well, to stretch out prone on his elbows with his view of the range at ground level, but not that of the cobalt sky above, partly blocked by more sticker brush and a clump of prickly pear just to his south.

He didn't care. He'd meant what he'd said to Clovinia about rising dust. There was just enough morning breeze to waft any powdery dust high and wide if any should be stirred out yonder. He smoked down his cheroot, decided against another, and stared sleepily at the clear cobalt-blue sky above the distant Candelarias until he found himself guarding the accused before the firm but fair Judge Dickerson of the Denver District Court, and neither His Honor nor that court stenographer seated across from him had had noticed he wasn't wearing a shirt.

He knew that once all hell broke loose, he'd have to leap to his feet and draw. But poor Miss Elsbeth, yonder; would never reproach him him for appearing before the bench so casually. For when the gun smoke cleared she'd be dead on the floor, with her notes on the proceedings scattered all to hell, and it would surely be a crying shame. For she was so pretty with that blond hair and eyes of cornflower blue, just as blue whether dead or alive.

As he braced himself for those desperados to shoot up the courtroom, Longarm had to wonder how come he was just sitting there, without a shirt, when he wasn't even on duty that morning. He suddenly recalled he hadn't been assigned to guard any prisoner. He'd only moseyed in to ask Elsbeth Flagg whether she'd like to drive out to Cherry Hill with him to watch the sun go down behind the Rockies, seeing she was new in town. As he stared wistfully across at her, knowing she'd be dead in a minute, he recalled how it was the dark eyed-Clovinia Spotted Deer who was blonde, while the blue-eyed Fran Baker's hair was black as midnight in a coal cellar. Then, just before they came in to kill her, the blue-eyed blonde in his dream asked, "Are you asleep, Custis?"

So Longarm said, "Not now," and woke up, lying on his side, to see Fran Baker had crawled in under the tented tarp beside him.

Wiping his sleep-gummed eyes, Longarm muttered, "For Pete's sake, we're in the open in broad daylight and I'll thank you to remember to call me Roger. Roger Tenkiller of the Cherokee Nation. Deputy Custis Long is dead. It says so in the papers, and what time is it? I was just dreaming about another federal official killed in the line of duty."

She said, "It's almost noon. I came up here to see if you'd like something to eat, and why can't I call you by your real name, seeing we're all alone over this way? Who's going to overhear us, and even if they did, most all those Cherokee know who you really are."

He said, "Loose lipping can lead to loose slipping when somebody *might* overhear you, and it's best to nip bad habits in the bud. As to whether I was hungry or not, I wasn't, until you woke me up. But now that I study on it, I reckon I could down some cold, canned beans with tomato preserves, or better yet, cold coffee."

She hesitated, reclining on one hip and elbow like Miss Cleopatra in that saloon painting, before she blurted out, "I'd like a few words with you in private first."

Longarm glanced down between their boots at the tree-tops rising from the shaded wash before he decided, "Well, with the others having grub together in the shade, with the sun glaring down as ferocious as it's fixing to get, I reckon we can chance it."

But when he hauled her in for a howdy kiss, she kissed back, startled, and then pulled away to gleep, "That's not what I wanted to ask about, you silly! It's high noon and anybody peering over the rim of that draw would be able to see under this tarp and up my skirts!"

"Not if we took everything off, ma'am," replied Longarm in a droll tone. "What did you want to talk about, if romance wasn't all you had in mind?"

She snapped, "I don't have that in my mind at all! Kiss Clovinia or one of those other squaws if you need to make love in broad daylight like a *critter*! I've been thinking about our earlier conversation, about Reverend Gibson having something up his sleeve."

Longarm shook his head and said, "We never had any such conversation. You'd figured out all by yourself that a dozen Cherokee were fixing to diddle your daddy's friends out of a thousand dollars to be divided a dozen ways. I told you how practical a motive that seemed."

She demurely replied, "What if the money we donated wasn't all they meant to smuggle into Mexico? I just managed a peek at the load just one of the pack ponies was toting as we jumped the border last night, thanks to you. At least one side of that packsaddle is packed with rifles, repeating Spencer rifles, and what do you have to say about that?"

Longarm said, "I'd have packed Winchesters or Henrys, at least, for them missionaries cut off to the south. Of course a rescue column would bring along extra guns and ammunition. What *else* would you want them to drag after them? Them Cherokee missionaries we're out to help already *have* Bibles printed in the so-called Sequoya alphabet. I fear you've been reading them sneaky books of Mr. Machiavelli, no offense. For once you get to brooding about all the two-faced tricks any suspect could possibly come up with, you just never can get to the bottom of the barrel. Let's go join the others for some grub. It's getting mighty hot up here, and nobody with human feelings would be yonder on them open flats at this hour."

Then, as he tossed the tarp aside and rose with his shirt in one hand to help her to her feet with the other, Longarm swore softly under his breath and added, "I'm sorry, Mr. Machiavelli. When you're right you're right, and I see there just *ain't* no bottom to the barrel of human contrariness!"

As he slipped on his shirt, the blue-eyed brunette asked what he was talking about. Longarm bent to pick up his hat and both guns as he muttered, "Look over yonder, a tad west of them crags on the southeast horizon, and see if you can guess!"

She shaded her eyes with one hand to stare into the shimmering heat waves above the flat expanse of low chaparral a spell before she told him, "I think I see trail dust, a more mustardy shade than the rest of the shimmer, and rising just a tad higher."

Longarm put on his hat after his .44-40 as he said, "You don't *think* a thing, Miss Fran. Somebody's out there, riding directly at us, sure as shooting!"

# Chapter 13

Horses ran much faster, trotted a little faster, but walked a little slower than a healthy man on foot. So it seemed to take forever for the four mounted figures coming in to be recognizable as three Mexican *peones* wearing white pajamas and big straw sombreros, escorting a Dominican nun in a black and white habit. The nun was naturally unarmed. The three men riding with her had single-shot musket-loaders across their thighs and machetes slung across their backs. All three were riding bareback with their bare feet hanging. The sister from what Longarm recalled as a teaching order sat ladylike in a proper side-saddle. She was the only rider sporting a bedroll and saddlebags behind her. The riders all gave the impression of having lit out from somewhere without taking time to pack all that much.

As the odd bunch got closer, Longarm called out to the others lined up along the rim of the wash, "Hold your fire and cover me. I suspect they're making a desperate dash for shade and don't know we're here."

Then he rose, leaving the Yellowboy on the ground and his six-gun in its holster, to stride out a few paces and wave his Stetson at them.

They reined in, as he'd expected, and held a tight, tense

conversation before one of the male Mexicans rode on in within earshot to call out, in Spanish, that he was an honest man guarding the life and virtue of Religiosa Catalina, bound for the military outpost at El Barreal.

Longarm called back in the same lingo that he was leading other honest Christians in the same direction, and invited them all to come in out of all that ferocious sunlight. So they did, and as they came closer he saw her escorts were kids and Sister Catalina, as you'd address her in English, was only a few years older. The oval olive face staring back at him with big sloe eyes that would have looked natural on a deer fawn was awesomely pretty for that infernal white robe and black wimple. She had to be sweating like a pig under all those duds. But she never let on as one of her young riders dismounted to help her and her own lathered pony down into the mesquite-shaded wash. The brown-haired Cherokee gal, Alice Bluejacket, ran over to hold out a canteen to Sister Catalina, who took it with a ladylike nod of thanks, put it delicately to her lips, and guzzled like a nursing shoat.

Up close, Sister Catalina smelled sort of like a pig as well. Once one of her Mex kids had put away half a canteen of water, he gasped, *"Muchas gracias,"* before he waved in the direction they'd just come from to tersely add, *"Escapamos los diablos indios de Victorio con minutas!"*

He didn't have to say much more. But Sister Catalina smiled up from her half-drained canteen to state in English, "You people are *americanos,* no? The village where another sister and I ran our small school was overrun last night by Apache. I owe my very life to these former students of mine. I don't know whether my companion, Sister Ynez, got away or not. If they have her, may a merciful God grant her a quick death! You people are running from Victorio too, no?"

Before Reverend Gibson or any of the others could mess up, Longarm said, *"Es verdad, mi religiosa Cata-*

*lina.* We were on our way to Ciudad Mejico along the usual *camino de correos* when some of your own folks warned us there were wild Indians ahead. So we swung over this way to see if we could just go around them, see?"

She answered, "No, I don't see. As we speak, Victorio and his many riders have occupied the high ground of La Candelaria, well this side of the patrolled postal route south."

Then she brightened and decided, "Oh, I *do* see! Like us, you think you will feel safer with those brave *federales* posted for to guard that water hole at El Barreal, no?"

Longarm hoped the others were following his drift as he calmly told her that was close enough, but added they'd been thinking of heading north for the border and their own cavalry at, say, Columbus until the excitement south of the border simmered down.

She said, "That Yanqui desert outpost named for Columbus, as you spell it, is much farther than El Barreal, and though why a just God should allow this escapes me, the Yaqui are said to be on the warpath as well, to the northwest."

Alice Bluejacket, backed by the more Indian-looking Margie McCash, invited the pretty but haggard nun to join them on a picnic blanket spread in heavier shade, and as she asked nobody in particular why they'd all been headed for Mexico City, Margie McCash, bless her forked tongue, calmly said she and the other ladies were tagging along after menfolk interested in government contracts. So Longarm knew she'd been paying attention earlier when he'd been explaining how Washington, Wall Street, and Rome had been lulled by El Presidente's soothing crime statistics and, in fairness, a tendency to pay folks Mexico owed money to. The late Benito Juarez had put needs such as irrigation projects, railroads, schools, and such ahead of paying off foreign investors and that, in a nutshell, had been what Maximilian had been all about.

Longarm could see that neither Sister Catalina nor her young rescuers had eaten recently, once the sisterly Cherokee ladies broke out more canned goods for them. He could see Reverend Gibson needed comforting at the moment. So he nodded at the old fuss and motioned to some other shade up the wash a ways. Old Todd Scraper and Stretch Tiawa tagged along until they were all well out of earshot. Longarm silently called a halt to their parade and turned to tell the Cherokee preacher, "There's no graceful way to keep that nun from reporting her narrow escape to the Mex military at El Barreal. They likely have a telegraph. Whether they have or not, they'll be anxious to spread the word about that other nun the Apache are holding, I hope."

Todd Scraper quietly asked, "Why do you palefaces always assume a white gal being held by Indians has to be getting raped?"

Longarm grimaced and snapped back, "That don't always happen, but it happens, so let's not bullshit about Mister Lo, the Poor Indian, with a gent who's scouted hostiles in his time. I'm sorry as all get-out about Sand Creek, and I'm willing to grant some Indian ladies were mistreated there by the Colorado Third. But let the record show the same innocent Cheyenne, shot up by the Third at Sand Creek, were holding three white women captive on the Washita when they got shot up by Custer and the Seventh Cav. All three had been raped, a lot. Or at least the two still able to communicate had. The third gal those poor innocent Cheyenne had captured had been driven out of her mind by the time that squaw-butchering Custer rescued her. The last I heard, she's still in an insane asylum back East. So could we get back to that more recently captured Mexican nun now?"

Todd Scraper didn't answer. Stretch Tiawa opined, "Say what you will about Cheyenne, George Armstrong Custer was a total cocksucker."

Todd Scraper laughed, and said, "Oh, come now, be

fair, we all know Old Yellowhair kept a harem of Cheyenne and Lakota *girls!*"

The tall, lean Tiawa calmly replied, "I stand corrected.
He was a total cuntlapper then."

The Reverend Gibson bristled, "Gentlemen, *please!* I'll
not have you use such language, even about George
Armstrong Custer!"

Tiawa grinned and asked, "Then what about dear old
Andrew Jackson, Rev?"

To which the Cherokee preacher replied without hesitation, "You mean our *utse-lv-nv-hi* who did so much for
us, Tseghsini? Well, as a Tsulagi-speaking man of the
cloth, I'll be charitable and just call him a motherfucking
thief!"

Then he smiled innocently at Longarm and added, "We
were speaking of that poor Mexican nun those Apache
captured. I don't suppose there's a thing we could do to
help her?"

Longarm said, "There ain't enough of us to even try.
If *los federales* get close enough in enough numbers to
matter, she'll only wind up dead for certain. If they ain't
killed her already, there's an outside chance she won't be
harmed all that bad."

"You mean they may not rape her?" asked the preacher
hopefully. Longarm shrugged and said, "Depends on your
definition of rape. She may say yes. Women can be flexible, given the choice of becoming the drudge of some
Na-déné women willing to take her as a slave or some
Na-déné buck offering to make her his play-pretty. I don't
think we ought to go into all that with Sister Catalina. We
have to send her on to those *federales* ignorant of *our*
intentions as well. So you might mention this in your own
lingo to everyone in your party, and I'll see Fran Baker
sticks to our story. Our story about being bound for Mexico City on business will be easier to stick to if nobody
volunteers any details nobody asks about. The game is
not to lie blatant enough to arouse suspicions, nor tell a

Catholic nun bound for a Mex military outpost about a Protestant mission that might not be on their map."

Longarm wasn't surprised when it was Todd Scraper who asked why they had to let Sister Catalina go. Longarm arched a brow when he dryly asked, "What was that I heard about us poor Indians catching hell about the treatment of white women?"

Scraper protested, "She ain't no whiter than the rest of us, and I never said anything about *hurting* her! I was just wondering why we couldn't just bring her along with us."

Longarm snorted. "How? There's four of them and fourteen of us if we count the gals. All bets would be off if even one escaped, and how tough might that be with all of us traveling at night on horseback? That would call for one guard to every prisoner, riding tight with guns drawn for night after night, with other things to worry our minds on every side. So I don't know about you, but figuring the guard roster for that much time on the trail is just too tedious for this child. I say let 'em go or kill 'em, and what's it going to be, Reverend Gibson?"

The Cherokee preacher gasped. "Killing even those boys would be out of the question! But what if they see through our masquerade and tell those Mexican soldiers about us?"

"Said *federales* may have enough on their plate with *wild* Indians. They may come after us. They may or may not cut our trail," Longarm replied with a fatalistic shrug.

Stretch Tiawa said, "They'll cut our trail. They'll only have to backtrack them four Mexican ponies to where they parted company with our twenty-eight, no matter where or when. I've hunted strays a single head at a time. So allow me to assure you twenty-eight shod ponies do not tread softly across desert pavement or alkali flats!"

Longarm made a mental note that the tall, lean Cherokee was another experienced cowhand, and declared, "I told you all back in El Paso it was going to be risky. The definition of risky is that you get to take risks. Since

105

we've agreed not to murder them innocent Mexicans in cold blood, we have to risk selling them some snake oil and letting them go."

So that was how they did it. Neither Sister Catalina nor her saviors had to be convinced it was too hot under the desert sun to ride on. So they lazed about, and from the way she smelled near supper time, Longarm knew some of the Cherokee gals had helped her out with some soap and water off in the mesquite a ways.

The four gals and other Cherokee men who hadn't been privvy to the staff meeting were taken discreetly aside at intervals. All agreed to stick to the same story, and nobody so far had told Sister Catalina or three kids who didn't speak English what was really going on.

The Mexicans, Sister Catalina included, were either delighted or polite about the canned beans and tomato preserves Fran Baker, being a Texas rider, had advised the Cherokee to stock up on back in El Paso. The fare could get tedious after four or five grub stops in a row, but as many an outfit witout a chuck wagon had learned the hard way, lots of other canned goods tasted worse eaten cold from the can, and some tended to seriously constipate a rider.

A mixture of pork and beans, tomato preserves, and cold coffee could last a long time. Monotonous trail grub didn't encourage ravenous appetites, so the rations lasted longer.

They all lazed amid the mesquites after supper, allowing the snakes to come out and slither about on the still-warm ground for a spell. Dudes might have wondered about that. But everyone in the party knew nearly all unprovoked rattlesnake bites took place during what both cowboys and Indians called the hour of the rattlesnake.

Scorpions were more inclined to sting you in the morning, when you put on the boot they'd crawled into to escape the chill of a desert night. Nothing cold-blooded moved around much after the sun had been down a spell.

So that was the best time to move in desert country.

They mounted up and rode out after nine P.M., breaking for ten minutes once an hour, and swapping saddles around two A.M. to give the pack ponies a break. That second night on the trail, not even the portly Reverend Gibson nor the good-sized Longarm weighed as much as a loaded packsaddle.

None of the Mexicans had to change mounts. Despite the lathering they'd taken escaping from the Candelaria Hills, their mounts had rested and browsed plenty of budding mesquite. Longarm had covered the same route before, riding in the opposite direction with Yaqui on his ass. So he navigated by desert stars so bright they looked as if you could stand in the stirrups and scoop them out of the sky with your hat, till he figured he was due north of those *federales* manning the outpost at El Barreal. He reined in beside Sister Catalina to ask her if she could point out the North Star. She laughed and pointed out that she was a schoolteacher. *"Por favor!"*

So, seeing she pointed to the North Star as well, Longarm told her, "This is where we go our separate ways, *mi religiosa*. If you and your *muchachos* ride straight across this open desert, keeping that one star directly behind you, you ought to make it into El Barreal no more than an hour or so after sunrise."

He couldn't read her pretty face by starlight after moonset, but her voice was smiling as she asked, "And what about you and your so kind friends? You will be riding toward that same star or another star leading perhaps another way?"

He said that was close enough, his conscience forcing him to toss in, "We may trend a tad to the west of due north. There's just more nothing on either side of the border due north."

She told him in that case to go with God, but insisted on a personal *adios* with each of the four gals who'd helped her freshen up before supper. Then she gathered

107

up her young riders to call out cheerfully, *"Vamanos pa'l carajo antes de que venga los indios!"* which was likely sincerely felt, coming from a nun. For it translated roughly as, "Let's get the hell out of here before those Indians show up!"

Her boys rode after her, laughing. Reverend Gibson reined in to one side of Longarm, Todd Scraper in tow. The Cherokee preacher asked how much time they had to work with.

To which Longarm could only reply, "All the time we need, if she bought our bullshit. We'd be over the horizon from the watchtower at El Barreal if this was broad day. By sunrise we ought to have made a good five miles to due west. If she didn't buy it, or those *federales* don't believe her, we're farther from any good place to hole up than she is from El Barreal, and there's no way in hell a blind man with a stick could avoid cutting the trail of twenty-eight ponies."

"We should have killed them," Todd Scraper muttered darkly.

Longarm's tone was only a tad more cheerful as he replied, "It's too late now. We'd best push on and put as much distance as we can betwixt our asses and *los federales* whilst we still have the time."

# Chapter 14

The old seaman's adage went: "Red sky at night, sailor's delight. Red sky in the morning, sailors take warning!" So Longarm was just as glad they were on higher ground when the sun rose like an egg yoke in tomato soup to catch them strung out like a line of ants on a pepper-sprinkled tablebloth.

Higher ground wasn't all that high as you rode deeper into the bottomlands of the Chihuahua desert. The mostly dead-flat dirty-white ground on all sides was the exposed caliche or desert pavement of wind-scoured gravel cemented by dry alkali. The pepper, or what looked like pepper at any distance, was the mostly greasewood and saltbush growing in scattered clumps. The change in the weather was both good and bad news.

As they rode on through the cool dawn, young Jim Whitemark overtook Longarm to point a little to the right of their course and ask if Longarm had ever seen such a realistic mirage before, with the sun behind them and the desert pavement tolerably cool.

Longarm replied, "That ain't no mirage. It's a real lake. Sort of. Miles across and inches deep. You get lakes like that in this part of the Chihuahua. I was afraid it was too early in the year to hope for playas. That's what the Mexicans call a desert lake dried out to 'dobe, flat as a pool table."

The Reverend Gibson rode up along his other side to ask, "Shouldn't we be headed for that water yonder? They tell me those waterbags we topped at that last stop are half empty now."

Longarm answered, "We'd best husband such water as we still have for the ponies. Had you asked me instead of Fran Baker, we'd be riding Spanish saddle mules. They can get by on about the same water rations as the rest of us. But what's done is done, and even if we don't make the Santa Maria before our waterbags are empty, it figures to rain. So we just might make it."

The Cherokee preacher protested, "But what about all that water in that lake over that way?"

Longarm said, "Might be just the ticket for doing laundry. You wouldn't want to *drink* it. And the lake's uncertain shore is rimmed with patches of quicksand, or liquid mud under a brittle, dry crust leastways. That there's the Laguna Guzman, and we don't want no part of it. I'm aiming to thread us through solid ground around the Laguna Santa Maria to our south. Once we're west of a smaller sink just as bad as the Guzman, we can circle on down to its source, the Santa Maria River, which runs across the desert something like the Humboldt up Nevada way, to peter out in its own wide and shallow sink."

The Reverend Gibson made a wry face and decided. "Well, our friends with Land Management told us you knew your way around Old Mexico. When and where do we make another day camp? I can see it hasn't gotten too hot yet. But our ponies have had a long night, and frankly, so has my poor old rump!"

Longarm said, "Welcome to the fraternity of serious riding. Them clouds in the east and the high water out ahead of us call for us to change our ways to fit the days. No offense, but Mister Lo, your poor Indian cousin, scared us palefaces before we noticed how often he used the very same tactics. The first couple of times the Comanche flattened out as the Texas Rangers fired a volley, rising again to charge in as they reloaded, worked like a charm. Then the Rangers got six-guns and orders not to fire in volley at the same time. But the Comanche never changed tactics that had worked so well in the past. Lord have mercy if a whole lot of Comanche didn't wind up dead."

"What about Custer at Little Big Horn?" Jim Whitemark dryly asked.

Longarm nodded and said, "Same deal. The books you read at West Point advise against dividing a regiment into more digestible bits. But Custer had found as early as the Peninsula Campaign of '62 that he was a brilliant cavalry leader. That's what you call a commander who bends the rules and surrounds the enemy a lot."

Heeling his mount onward, Longarm conceded, "A two-pronged attack with a third of his riders in reserve to back up the prong that made contact had worked for him again and again before he tried it at Little Big Horn. But Benteen led the reserve column to back Reno on *his* ridge, instead of Custer on his. They'd have surely court-martialed Old Yellowhair instead of Reno if it had gone down in the books as Reno's Last Stand."

The Reverend Gibson said, "Thank you for the pointless history lesson, and we're still going to end up hot and weary!"

Longarm replied, "Not as hot as we'd likely wind up if we stopped out here on this sunbaked caliche to day-camp. The point I was out to make is that you can't keep doing the same things under different conditions. You'll thank me do we make sweet water and more shade by the time we're really hurting!"

So they rode on, and on. Then Longarm called a trail break, adding, "Dismount and water the stock. But only let them have a quart this time, and don't drink any your ownselves."

He replied to the collective grumble with: "It's all right to sip any coffee you have left in your canteens. But don't open any cans of tomato preserves if you were planning on your regular noon meal!"

As he dismounted himself, Fran Baker joined him, swatting flies off her boot tops with her riding crop, or leastways, swatting. She told him, "I'm not sure we have a quart of water left for each and every pony."

Longarm said, "Sure you have. I've been keeping score. We ought to have at least two hundred pounds or better than thirty *gallons* of of water left, unless someone's been pouring water on the ground."

Fran sighed and said, "Someone's been pouring water on the ground. Me and the other girls had to let that poor nun use just enough water to soap up and rinse off all over back in that last day camp. It's too delicate to discuss with menfolk, but she was in a bad way, after riding so hot and sweaty during her . . . time of the month. One of those Cherokee girls did say you'd never approve of emptying that whole waterbag. But we all agreed we had to. So I guess we never asked."

Longarm laughed despite himself and said, "I'm just as glad you never asked permission. I'd have been in a real pickle, having to decide, in view of the poor gal's dire need."

He thought, shrugged, and said, "Well, what's done is done and as long as Sister Catalina is no longer with us, I don't have to order you ladies not to do that anymore. So let's see about watering these poor thirsty brutes with such water as we still have."

As they were doing so, off to the northwest of the military outpost at El Barreal, Sister Catalina and her brave students were being met on the open flat by a corporal's squad of gray-uniformed *federale* lancers, alerted by the guard tower.

"Now remember, *muchachos*," the teaching sister was telling her former grammar school pupils, "we shall tell those *soldados* the truth about those Apache overrunning your village. We shall beg them for to save poor Religiosa Ynez if she is still alive. But I wish to hear no more nonsense about those *americanos* who helped us being Indians!"

"But they were !" insisted the sharp-eared Jesus Valdez, who'd overheard duskier members of the gringo party conversing in what sounded like Gulf Coast Caddo to him. He told the Dominican nun, "I know they were not Apache, Religiosa Catalina. Like my grandmother's Laguneros, the Caddo are honest, farming people who have no use for those Apache.

But I still say those gringos were *gringos indios*, or most of them were. Some few might have been pure *blanco*. What does it matter?"

Sister Catalina said, "Listen to me, Jesus. It may matter a good deal. I don't know why those young women lied to me, even as they treated me so kindly. But the point is that they *were* very kind to us all, even as I too overheard things I may not have been supposed to overhear."

"What do you think they are really up to, Religiosa Catalina?" asked the darker and more thoughtful Hernan.

The nun shrugged and said, "I don't know. I choose not to concern myself. I know they were poor misguided *protestantes* who behaved as true Christians to members of a rival faith, and did I not teach you *muchachos* the parable of the Samaratino Bueno?"

When none of them argued, she waved to the oncoming lancers and told the kids with her, "We were helped by an *americano* party fleeing from Victorio as well. They told us they had been on their way to Ciudad Mejico on business, but the last we saw of them they were riding back to their own country and that is all we have to say about them!"

Meanwhile, off to the northwest, Longarm and the others were on their way, trending southwest again, having circled El Barreal and, with any luck, the treacherous Laguna Santa Maria. Longarm had no intention of riding close enough to open water surrounded by square miles of sun-crusted salt marsh to make certain.

The overcast sky to the east helped a bit. It wasn't as hot this late in the morning as it would have been on a clearer desert day. But the ponies were tired and thirsty past their reliable limits. Humans and even dogs could carry on despite feeling just awful. Horses were inclined to go crazy when they felt bad, and it didn't feel good to trudge on mile after mile, dying for a drink of water.

So, next trail break, Longarm ordered their nose bags filled with all the water left, explaining, "Water weighs eight pounds a gallon, and they'll feel better with it in their guts instead of aboard their packsaddles. After that we're in a whole lot of trouble if I'm lost, and within hours of sweet water if I ain't."

When Fran Baker commented about cutting their luck mighty thin, he shrugged and replied, "That's what I just said."

They rode on and on, and first one pony, then a second, foundered under its load and just lay there on the caliche, waiting to be put out of its misery.

But there was more than one way to skin a cat or cope with a worn-out pack pony. So Longarm had first one, then the other relieved of its pack, and just left the packs there beside the ponies as the expedition pressed on. One of the abandoned ponies got right to its feet to follow them, bareback, plaintively neighing for them to wait up.

As Longarm explained, once they made it to more water they could send somebody back with refilled waterbags to fetch that other pony and both packsaddles. When someone asked what happened if they didn't reach sweet water all that soon, he could only say that those foundered brutes would be the least of their problems.

Over in El Barreal Sister Catalina was having her own problems with the ambitious over-age-in-grade commander of the *federales* posted out in the middle of nowhere much.

Seated in his office, he'd politely but stubbornly made the Dominican nun go over her story again and again. So once again Sister Catalina was saying, "I assure you I have told you all I can, *mi capitán*. The *americanos* we encountered out on this desert were not only most kind, but literally saved out lives. We were forced to flee Victorio with neither food nor enough water to carry us through this far. They took us in for to share their food and water with us more than freely. They offered me enough water for to *bathe* myself, even though I protested they could not have that much water for to spare. Is true I needed a bath very badly. But I would have survived without one if they had not insisted, and I shall always remember them with gratitude and love!"

The lancer captain nodded understandingly and said, "We have wired the sad news about that other *religiosa* the Apaches may be holding to our Chihuahua headquarters. If Victorio remains in La Candelaria long enough, our mountain artillery will no doubt persuade him he should have allowed Los Yanquis to move him and his ragged followers to that new reservation north of the Gila."

Sister Catalina blanched and anxiously demanded, "But what about poor little Ynez, and those other Christian women the Apaches may be holding? Will not artillery fire present as great a danger to them as to them their Apache captors?"

The captain replied, soberly but not unkindly, "Probably *more* danger to any captives in their cramped camping grounds. Apache women and children may be killed in greater numbers than experienced warriors who know for how to take cover at short notice. Is simply the way one must make war on an enemy who brings his women, children, and of course any captives into the field of battle with him."

115

The captain was a professional soldier, not a naturally cruel man. So he understood the bewildered tears in the pretty nun's eyes as he continued with the relentless logic of military science. "No soldier raised by decent people wishes for to commit atrocities. No soldier committed to winning can *avoid* committing atrocities against *Indians*. I was one of those few cadets who survived the Yanqui attack on what they now like to call the Halls of Montezuma. They butchered us like cattle. It was dreadful, and at the time I felt sure the fiends of hell had killed most of my young comrades and brushed the rest of us away like flies."

"I have heard of the massacre of Chapultepec," said Sister Catalina as she made the sign of the cross.

The lancer captain shrugged and said, "Now that I am an old *soldado,* I can say with some assurance that had I been in command on the other side at Chapultepec, I'd have butchered those poor stupid cadets just as ruthlessly. We were only boys. Was our first taste of battle. We should have known our situation was hopeless when the regulars all ran away. But we stood our ground against Yanqui shot and shell and cold cold steel, and they too did what they had to do. Is no way at such a time to single out who is an innocent in your way and who may be about to kill you. Is not our fault, nor the fault of *Los Yanquis,* much as I hate to say it, that *Los indios* choose to fight us with women and children riding along. If they do, they die, and the sooner is all over, the sooner *nobody* will have to die."

He shook himself as if to get back on track, and told the nun, "Is no matter. My own patrol will not be riding toward any Apache over in La Candelaria. I am only sending them north to see which way those kindly gringos rode after they parted ways with you, *comprende?*"

Sister Catalina almost wailed, "For why? I told you they told me they were riding back to their own country, *mi capitán!*"

He nodded soberly and replied, "I know what they told you. I have to make certain they were telling you the truth. I have received anxious wires about a mysterious gringo party of perhaps a dozen who told yet another Mexican lady of quality a great lie the other night!"

# Chapter 15

Deep-rooted mesquite didn't thrive where the water table was close enough to the sky for faster-sprouting trees to flourish. So once the rescue mission had made it far enough upstream along the west bank of the northward-flowing Santa Maria, the tanglewood along either bank of the braided desert stream was mostly willow and cotton-wood. Both gave tolerable shade. But ponies only browsed cottonwood, because willow leaves tasted like medicine.

Longarm let his human followers and their critters rest up in the shade by sweet waters for a spell, but warned them not to spread their bedding that close to the now-shallow Santa Maria, with all those dark clouds hanging almost still in the eastern sky.

When Fran Baker came slapping at her boots to point out the *afternoon* sky was likely to wind up sunny and warm indeed, Longarm said, "I hope not. We could use a good gully-washer to hide the clear trail we've had to leave across all that crunchy caliche. An inch or more of rain might save us a lot of bother with *los federales*, but it could turn yonder river into a serious problem whilst it was at it. So when we settle into this day camp, we'd best do so on that higher ground to the west, above the floodplain of this occasional imitation of the Arkansas these Cherokee folks know better."

The Reverend Gibson, close enough to hear, turned to complain, "That rise is a quarter mile away from this shade, and I thought you said we'd be traveling by day now."

Longarm said, "We'll tote some shade over yonder with us. Roofing, improvised from cottonwood saplings and willow branches, offers shade galore for our critters and us, and better shelter than these treetops if it really rains. As for moving by day or by night in uncertain times and places, I thought I'd explained that we have to be flexible. We want to be able to watch our steps tight as we work our way through these treacherous but mostly uninhabited lowlands. Once we're high and dry enough to be spotted from the higher Sierras further west, we'll want to be moving at night some more."

Nobody argued the point further, and by the time Whitemark and old Todd Scraper had returned with all the foundered ponies and abandoned packsaddles, Longarm and the others had gotten to work on a much more substantial day camp of lean-tos great and small. The spent ponies, party restored already by canteen water carried back to them, seemed to be bouncing back after a wallow in the sandy shallows and some good chaws of fresh-sprouted cottonwood leaves.

As he was tying the last willow branches to his ridge-pole, since you thatched such a roof from the ground up so each new row would overlap the one below it, Fran Baker came over to ask him if he didn't think this modest trail town they were erecting might not be visible a long ways off.

Longarm nodded, but asked, "Who to? We're miles from that nearest military outpost, with two wooded riverbanks between. As you gaze over to the west, them purple mountains peeping over the horizon are too far for anyone peering east across this desert to make us out with field glasses."

"What about a telescope? Like that Eye-talian professor used to make out them canals on the planet Mars?" she asked.

Longarm laughed and said, "If the Yaqui dwelling over in them purple mountains have an astronomical observatory, and ain't pointing it up, we may be in an awful fix. You missed the lecture on field tactics I was giving earlier. But time's a-wasting, and I'll thank you to just remember there's no such thing as an absolutely sure bet, and if you can't live with them odds you have no business betting at all. Do you need any help with your own shelter, ma'am?"

She said she didn't and stomped off, whipping her boot top like it had done her wrong.

Having finished his triangular thatched hut, or pup tent of willow branches, depending on how you wanted to describe it, Longarm spread his bedding atop the ground-cloth carpeting most of the inside, and shucked his shirt, hat, and gunbelt to crawl in for some shade, since the sun had now peeked over those thunderheads that didn't seem to be going anywhere.

Thunderheads behaved that way in the southwest or northern Mexico, depending on whom one asked. The dry, sunny climate was inspired some by mountains blocking off most rain clouds from the Pacific Ocean or Gulf of Mexico, but mainly by the simple fact it didn't rain much at that latitude.

Western deserts such as the Mojave and Sonora could count on some good winter rains off the Pacific. East of the Continental Divide the winter rains never arrived, and such summer rains as you got came in off the Gulf when they damn well felt like it. When rain did hit the desert from the east, it tended to make up for all that tedious sunshine with really awesome downpours and plenty of hail and thunderbolts thrown in.

Meanwhile, now that the damned sun was closer to the

zenith in the clear two thirds of the cobalt sky, it was already commencing to feel stuffy under all those wilting willow leaves. He could only take some comfort in knowing cottonwood leaves had far more moisture in them.

Given the choice of shucking everything and lying under one flannel blanket, or keeping his underdrawers on for modesty, he elected to stretch out atop the covers in his cotton underdrawers, and if anybody peeked, it would serve them right.

He still felt funny a few minutes later when the brown-haired Miss Alice Bluejacket ducked in with him, hesitated at the sight of his bare feet and naked chest, and allowed she'd come to say she was sorry.

Longarm rose on one elbow to pat a space beside him as he assured her she had nothing to be sorry about as far as he could see.

Hunkering on her knees beside him, the Cherokee gal, who looked far more Anglo-Saxon than the dark-haired and weathered Longarm, said she was sorry because it had been her notion to waste all that water on that one nun. She said, "None of us have been able to really . . . clean ourselves since that last town. So I don't suppose it would have really hurt Sister Catalina if she'd had to go another day without a bath and . . . freshening."

Longarm said, "You ladies done right. It wouldn't have hurt her fatal, but she was doubtless uncomfortable as all get-out. I've . . . ah, heard about some of the sanitary problems you ladies have on occasion."

He saw he'd said too much when the churchgoing Cherokee gal blushed beet red and crawfished backwards out of his shelter to run off without a word of good-bye. No words of explanation had been needed.

Longarm muttered, "When will you learn that some folks have prissy notions about the simple facts of nature? Wasn't it a grown *man* of the British persuasion who shot that boy in Leadville for intimating they had to have a shithouse somewhere in Buckingham Palace?"

He adjusted his hardware, fashioned a pillow from his hat and shirt, and lay back down for a lazy stretch. Then the Cherokee blonde, old Clovinia Spotted Deer, crawled in wearing a fresh red calico frock, flopped beside him, and sobbed, "I have to know, for I'm a natural woman with natural feelings. What on earth do you *do* to women, you sly dog?"

Longarm replied innocently and truthfully that he didn't know what in blue blazes she was talking about.

She said, "Oh, come now. I was at the Eagle Hotel the other night, and you can't tell me you didn't make that Mexican girl come more than once."

Longarm smiled sheepishly and explained, "That was in the line of duty, Miss Clovinia. It don't take no special skills to make love to a spy-gal who's been ordered to make love to you in her own line of duty."

Clovinia insisted, "I could tell that she enjoyed it. I was right outside your door when you brought her to climax more than once. At the risk of having you low-rate me, I am not without experience in such matters. I've been . . . engaged more than once. The reason I broke off with more than one swain was simply because they failed to . . . you know how some men fail some women. So tell me what you could have *done* to Fran and Alice, within the hour, to send them away looking so . . . ravaged!"

Longarm laughed sincerely and said, "You have my word as an enlisted man but a gentleman that I never did no such thing to either of them other ladies!"

She nodded soberly and calmly replied, "I wouldn't expect you to kiss and tell. I like that in a man."

So he kissed her, and she kissed back in a way to make him believe she'd been failed a time or more.

Then she pushed away to breathlessly gasp, "For heaven's sake, it's going on high noon and you built no *ends* on this silly little hut!"

Longarm neither fought to hang on to her nor pushed her away as they reclined side by side. He said, "It would be even stuffier in here if I'd tried to build ends on this double lean-to. As to the time you chose, I never picked it, no offense. But I see your point. Sort of. You'd have heard me tell old Gibson we'll try to get on across this desert by moonlight, come moonrise. But there's always another time and place, Miss Clovinia, and sometimes things work out just as well when the time and place seems unfitting and you have to hold your horses till your horse sense catches up."

She sighed and asked, "What if he or she who hesitates is lost and there never comes a fitting time and place?"

He said, "When things are meant to happen, there's almost always a time and place. When folks have second thoughts, it's usually just as well if they don't."

She sat up in the humidily cozy shelter and said, "I know. Let's go swimming!"

Longarm laughed and said, "Miss Clovinia, the Santa Maria's mighty wide, but hardly deep enough for swimming."

To which she demurely replied, "Oh, I don't know. I'm sure we could find a place deep enough for you if we felt around for it."

Longarm laughed, and might have implied she'd gone *loco en la cabeza* if he hadn't wondered why any natural man would want to say a silly thing like that. So he kissed her some more, and in no time at all they were bound for the wooded banks of the nearby Santa Maria. And if anybody noticed, they didn't see fit to raise a fuss about it.

Once they were out of sight in the tanglewood, Clovinia kissed him again and led him by the hand through the greenery until they were a furlong or more upstream of the camp. When they came to an open patch of orchard grass barely big enough to spread a picnic blanket, Clovinia calmly shucked her red summer frock over her blond head and, kneeling in the dappled shade in all her naked glory, spread the red calico on the springy grass as Longarm hung his gunbelt over a cottonwood branch to get himself to the same state of nature.

By the time he had, Clovinia was supine on her calico, spread-eagled and blond all over, with her eyes squeezed shut like a kid getting set to take her medicine. So he dropped to his bare knees between her wide-spread shins and eased forward atop her to give her a dose of his old organ-grinder.

Her hot, moist ring-dang-doo sent contrary messages as she opened her eyes to protest, "My God! What are you *doing* to me?"

Since she was doing it to him at the same time, with rapid-fire hip thrusts, it seemed too dumb a question to answer. So he just kissed her some more and returned her tacit compliments with hard thrusts of his own while being careful not to slam her tailbone against the firmer than usual bedding with his full weight. For he knew, as she could no doubt feel then and there, that part of the trouble brides complained of after a disappointing wedding night was that beds were far softer than the mother earth the human race had screwed on for a mighty long time before anyone had invented a mattress. So the clitoris had evolved, as Professor Darwin put the process, to be thumped by a gent's public bone against the gal's pubic bone as they fornicated, braced at the right thumping angle by a firmly backed tailbone. But of course, one of the reasons the mattress had been invented was that men tended to overdo such pounding when a gal was really inspiring, and there was something about a naked dark-eyed blonde with firmly bouncing breasts and just a hint of wild Indian about her that made it hard not to drive his hard-on deep enough to kill her.

But Longarm was considerate and experienced enough to satisfy himself in a gal without doing her bodily harm, and Clovinia, it seemed, was experienced enough to come ahead of him twice, in spite of all that bullshit about other men.

He'd never figured out why women were more inclined than men to brag on previous fucking. Most men figured few gals wanted to hear tell of other such incidents, and most men were right. But he was braced for a tale of woe about some shiftless skunk who'd done her wrong as they had to stop and come up for air.

But this time she murmured, "Oh, Custis, I mean Roger, I feel so low. I never should have let you do this to me!"

He asked if she'd like him to take it out, and she hugged him in tighter with her crossed legs, even as she sobbed, "You know I don't. But it's wrong, wrong, wrong in the eyes of the Lord!"

Longarm moved his hips to soak it at a more comfortable angle as he dryly remarked, "That sounds reasonable. He who made the lion and the lamb, the sun and stars, to set the planets in their courses, must be staring down right now to gasp at the sight of two mortals having a piece in the bushes!"

She laughed, accused him of pure sophistry, and asked if she could get on top. So he let her as, out to the north on those open flats, a pair of riders who could have been taken for Mexican *vaqueros* a ways off had reined in to stare soberly down at the considerable sign left by twenty-eight shod ponies across desert pavement.

But up close they were conversing in Nauatl as they agreed on either a pack train or a *federale* column.

Finally, the older of the two young scouts decided, "We waste time asking questions of the wind. Let us ride back to tell the others of these tracks. It is up for them to decide what to do about them."

His younger companion smiled wolfishly and asked, "What is there to decide? We are Yaqui, not effeminate *cristianos* who squat to' piss and think twice about what should be done to strangers!"

# Chapter 16

The moon likely rose at its appointed time that night, but it was tough to tell, at first, because of those threatening clouds off to the east as they rode south along the Santa Maria. Around about midnight they heard what sounded like a rumble of thunder in the distance, but the star-spangled sky above stayed clear and dry till dawn.

By that time they'd made better than twenty more miles, and the desert pavement away from the river was peppered with more substantial although low chaparral as they left the more alkaline bottomlands.

The hot, sunny day passed much as the one before had, including a "swim" with old Clovinia. By nightfall the sky was once more a cloudless blue bowl from horizon to horizon, with the horizon the sun was setting behind the jagged sawtooth outline of the Sierra Madre Occidental, which meant "Mother's Western Saw," the Mexicans' likely meaning the mother of God.

When Longarm felt it was time to part company with the Santa Maria, lest it lead them to another military outpost at the riverside town of Galeana, he led them in a direction that surprised them some, back across the shallow river and then on up to an island in the sky called the Sierra de las Tunas or Prickly Pear Ridge. Actually, a little pinyon pine and juniper grew on the higher crags of the fault block, a good seventy-five miles long north to south, but barely five miles across, with open desert to its east or west.

Longarm told the others how he'd ridden the same ridge alone, for his life, in earlier times of trouble south of the border. So he knew that while Indians, Christian or pagan, might wander over to gather pine nuts and tunas, or cactus fruit, in season, there was no call for anyone to build a village along the Sierra de las Tunas, and so nobody ever had.

Seeing that they'd spent the night before in their saddles, Longarm told them he thought it best they run the ridge as far as their ponies were able, day-camp by the one game trail along the crest, and then stay safely put the following night to try for an early start by dawn light. When the Reverend Gibson objected to all the time they'd lose by camping more than twelve hours, Longarm pointed out that a horse and rider tumbling off a cliff in the dark could lose far more than twelve hours out of their collective lives.

He explained, "You may have noticed this ridge ain't heavily wooded, and when it does rain up here it rains serious enough to carve steep and deep. So we want to watch where we're riding, and thanks to all of this high cactus to either side of the trail, nobody down below to either side is likely to spot us."

Fran Baker was the one who asked, "What about our dust?"

He told the blue-eyed brunette, "That's another reason I chose to follow this route for a spell. Desert deer and bighorns have paved this narrow trail along the ridge solid as cement with thousands and thousands of hoofbeats. As long as we walk our mounts along the ridge, we won't raise enough dust to clear the cactus tops. So I figure we ought to make good time and cover some distance in the next two or three days."

Somebody else asked where they'd be when they ran out of a lonesome ridge to run. Longarm said, "We'll come down the far end into milpas around the village of Bachiniva, alongside that Santa Maria River to our west."

Reverend Gibson protested, "But didn't we just ford the Santa Maria to avoid such river towns?"

Longarm nodded and said, "We did. Above Bachiniva we'll ford her some more, streak due west across such desert as we'll find that far upstream, and streak for tall timber in the front ranges of the higher Sierra Madres over yonder. That'll put us a within a little over two hundred miles of that cut-off Cherokee mission, with all the wilder Indians and most of the trouble they've stirred up well behind us."

He paused, grimaced, and added, "I'm still working on how we get our fool selves and anyone we rescue back to the border through more of the same. But you can only eat an apple a bite at a time. So why don't we move on down the pike to the Rio Verde?"

Nobody argued. So he took the point and led them single file along the narrow game trail between high walls of prickly pear, or *tuna* if you wanted to define that particular Mex subspecies.

All cactus of the *opuntia* or prickly pear tribe rose short or tall as jointed stems that looked like chains of flat green powder puffs being used as pincushions. From the tiny specimens growing on the high plains of Wyoming and even the dunes of Cape Cod to the eight- or-ten-foot *tunas* all around, they all sprouted flowers that looked like roses of different colors in the spring and set spiny, seedy, albeit mighty sweet red fruit from high summer into fall. Longarm had read somewhere how professors thought most every sort of New World cactus could trace its lineage back to a wild desert rose.

He didn't care. What he liked most about prickly pear was that you could hide out in it when it grew tuna-sized. So once the sun rose high enough to bake their narrow trail and some of the gals were really starting to bitch about feeling saddlesore, Longarm called a halt near a natural break in the cactus east of the trail, and led them all through it and down the slope a ways.

"In the rare event that anyone should come along that trail we just left," he said, "they shouldn't notice if we bust our way into this cactus on the the downhill side. Keep track of the pads you break off. When you have time, a peeled cactus pad tastes like an apple or a turnip to your ponies. We ought to split up and hollow out single nests we can roof over easier by bending the tops together and spreading tarps or saddle blankets across the gap. You'll find them handy stable stalls as well as shelters, come rain or shine."

So that was what all of them did, as best they could, with some doing better than others, but nobody flunking the course totally because it hardly took a degree in architecture once you had a wall of cactus to either side. The stuff grew naturally in hedgerows a yard or more apart, with the bare soil between sucked too dry by shallow cactus roots for anything else to sprout.

As he was putting the finishing touches on his own hidey-hole he was joined by the Cherokee blonde, Clovinia, who said, "Custis, we have to talk."

Some wise old sage had recorded that when a woman said you and she had to talk, she expected you to listen tight while she did all the talking. So Longarm just went on spreading his bedding, and sure enough, she said, "I'm afraid we're going to have to be more . . . discreet from now on."

She said some of the other gals had been commenting on a Cherokee church lady sparking so openly with a white man they'd never seen in their Cherokee church. Longarm had noticed, staring down between their bare bellies in motion now and again, how dumb a dicusssion about their complexions would be. But he assured the Cherokee gal with whiter hide than his own that he understood her concerns for her reputation, and agreed it might be best if they were just friends for a spell.

They parted friendly, and Longarm was feeding his ponies peeled cactus pads as juicy as watermelon rind when the brown-haired Miss Alice Bluejacket tracked him down and allowed they had to talk.

But she didn't want to say she didn't cotton to a romance with a shiftless white boy. She asked him to repeat what he'd said about them having two hundred miles or more to go.

When he said he was being optimistic, and agreed it might take as much as another two weeks on the trail, she told him their canned grub would never last them that long, and asked what they could do.

Longarm said, "I'll talk to Reverend Gibson. Do we still have rations for, say, a week?"

She shook her head and said, "Three days at the most. And won't we be coming back with *more* mouths to feed?"

He said, "We'll have to pick up more trail supplies in, let's say, Bachiniva to be safe. Safer than riding into Ciudad Guerrero least ways. There's a *federale* headquarters garrison in Ciudad Guerrero, which means Warrior City."

She said, "But I heard you tell Reverend Gibson you wanted to lead us *around* that river crossing at Bachiniva, and where will we ever find canned goods in a Mexican village?"

He said, "You have to play the cards Lady Luck deals you. So we'll have to risk riding into Bachiniva instead of riding around it, and you buy canned goods in a Mexican village at their *abaceria* or grocery store, of course. This may come as a shock to you, Miss Alice, but we didn't invent canned goods. The notion started in the Old World and sort of spread. So Mexican canned goods are labeled in Spanish, but they have to be just as free of bugs. Cans explode when you fail to kill all the bugs in the cans you're cooking under steam pressure."

She seemed dubious. Reverend Gibson didn't cotton to the notion much, until Longarm assured him prices would be much lower in Mexico. So they all crawled into their cactus caves for a spell, and it was just as well they did because it commenced to rain fire and salt.

After dark Clovinia came back, saying that all that thunder had spooked her and allowing she might not have meant *totally* discreet.

But another wise old sage had written, doubtless in French, that a man who didn't quit while he was ahead was a jack-off who deserved to wind up wedding the gal of his nightmares.

So he sent her back to her own cactus cave rain-soaked and wet-eyed, and they got going the next day to run the ridge by daylight. And so it went for the next few days on the trail, until they were running out of ridge, beans, and tomato preserves at about the same time.

Longarm had been studying the cards Lady Luck had dealt out. So when they passed the first goat herds and came upon the outlying corn milpas around the village of Bachiniva, he called a halt and told the others it might be best if most of them stayed put while he, their leader, and half the men led the pack ponies into town to pick up fresh trail supplies.

He explained, "That rain may have washed out our tracks to the north, and you can see they don't have a telegraph line out this way. But we want them to recall us as a bunch of Anglos, not a larger party with four women in it. So we'd best make a day camp over in yonder grove of mesquite and tiptoe in after La Siesta, in the tricky light of sundown, to spread some *dinero* and leave a sweet aftertaste as we go round 'em after dark."

They agreed that made sense and followed him east, away from the village and riverbank, into the mesquite in the middle distance he'd indicated.

Some men and boys from the village naturally drifted

out to ask if they could be of any service. Longarm saw all four gals had been smart enough to shade on the far side of the tethered twenty-eight ponies. None of the Cherokee men were dumb enough to be rude to the nosey villagers. They followed Longarm's lead as he doled out smokes and regretfully confessed they were low on grub. The Mexicans lit out before they could be expected to invite any *gringos chingados* to supper, if that was what the tall one had been hinting at.

Longarm made everyone sit tight during the tedious four hours of the midday siesta. It was too blamed hot to wander around in the sun in any case. That was the point of La Siesta.

As he lounged on the sand with his back to a mesquite trunk and a cheroot in his teeth, Fran Baker came over to pester him some more about infernal Cherokee out to sell her daddy and those other Texicans a gold brick. Considering all her harebrained confidence games helped him pass the time. But it still seemed a million years before Longarm felt it was time to mosey on in.

The Cherokee preacher was fidgety as a little kid trying not to piss his pants. But when he ordered Todd Scraper to saddle up at least eight pack mules, Longarm warned, "One bite at a time, Rev. You don't put on a show in a small town unless you're going to put on a circus. You, me, and say two of the boys ought to drift in first, belly up to the bar in the cantina, and get to talking friendly with some locals before we casually mention we could use some canned goods. One of the locals is sure to owe money and favors to the owner of the *abaceria,* and you'll find the prices more reasonable, and we'll answer fewer questions, if they ask *us* to do business with *them,* see?"

The preacher did, even though he didn't hold with drinking. Longarm assured him he'd be proud to drink *his* tequila too. So the four of them mounted up and walked their ponies into town.

Longarm had passed through before. But he'd have

hardly needed to ask directions to the one cantina fronting on the one dirt-paved plaza. He nodded politely to such staring faces as they passed, and it only felt as if they'd ridden a hundred miles by the time they reined, tethered up, and stepped into the cooler *cerveza*-scented interior of the cantina.

As they did so, they saw nobody had lit any candles as yet, and the cloudless red sky outside didn't cast enough light through the door and two windows to matter. But Longarm recalled where the bar was and led the way, nodding to the dim outlines of the portly barkeep and an even less noticeable figure down at one end on their side of the bar.

Longarm asked if the barkeep recalled him from his last visit, and when the Mexican replied with a flat lie and a friendly nod, Longarm said, "*Bueno,* in that case we'll have four tequilas, and why don't you have one with us?"

When the barkeep agreed to have a shot on them, Longarm turned to the darker figure down the way to ask in a friendly tone, "What about you, *caballero*? Would you join us for a drink?"

The fuzzy blackness at the end of the bar calmly replied, "*Muchas gracias, pero no.* I have a full glass, El Brazo Largo. Have you heard the bounty on your head is now ten thousand pesos?"

# Chapter 17

"It's all right! Hold your fire!" Longarm snapped as he detected the twang of tensed gun hands around him. Then, seeing the cantina seemed nigh empty and the barkeep had to be in with La Causa Libertad if they were free to use Longarm's Mexican nickname, Longarm nodded to the sinister outline. "Evening, El Gato. What brings you to this wide spot on a desert trail?"

El Gato, as the handsome young man of pure Spanish lineage, with the outfit of a prosperous *vaquero* with a taste for black leather, was called, chuckled fondly and replied, "I was about to ask you the same thing. I knew you would be coming up the river or along the Sierra de las Tunas if it was you. I was almost certain it was you when we got word about that most amazing gunfight up near the Laguna Santa Maria."

Longarm introduced the Mexican rebel leader, or bandit, depending on who one asked, to the three Cherokee with him, assuring them El Gato, or The Cat, wasn't so called because you wanted to pet him. He was a natural freak of nature who could somehow see in the dark like a cat, and could draw like a grocery-store mouser could pounce. El Gato told them he'd heard about their expedition. La Causa had its own spies working for the nationalized telegraph network.

Longarm said, "Never mind about us. We figured they figured we'd jumped the border. What was that about an amazing gunfight they have me down for now? Refresh my memory. I just can't recall having such a gunfight with anybody."

El Gato moved close enough for them to see he'd arched a brow as he replied, "*Es verdad?* I felt sure it had to be true when I heard of a ten-man lancer patrol and over a dozen Yaqui scattered across a playa in various states of disrepair. *Los federales* feel someone somehow invited Indians fighters and Indians to the same dance, for to show everybody a wild time indeed."

Longarm thought back, nodded, and decided, "I see what must have happened. I take it *los federales* ain't been able to backtrack them Yaqui, or cut the trail of anybody *they* were tracking?"

El Gato shook his head, wagging his awesome black sombrero, as he replied, "*Pero no*. Was a *temporal grander,* I mean one big thunderstorm, the evening of the battle. Washed away a lot of blood and all the hoofprints leading in or out of the dolorous panorama. When the patrol never returned, the relief column was led to their bodies by the, how you say, vultures? Yaqui like for to come back for their own dead, if any get away alive. So the feeling is both sides were wiped out by somebody worse, who rode off laughing in the rain."

Longarm made a wry face and muttered, "Never pass on a complicated explanation when a simple one will do. Many a man's gotten off a few rounds after he's been mortally gutshot."

El Gato nodded soberly and mused, "That would make *me* mad enough to shoot somebody. But when the legend seems more amusing than the truth, let us pass along the legend. What makes you so mean, El Brazo Largo?"

Longarm answered dryly, "Nerves, I reckon. Since

you're so nosey, *amigo mio,* me and these other gringos are trying to get down to the headwaters of the Rio Verde, high in the hills to the southwest of San Francisco del Oro. How do you like it so far?"

The Mexican in black downed his tequila neat, not screwing around with lemons or salt the way they did in border towns, and told them, "You do not wish for to ride that far. Is no longer *necesario.*"

"You mean our friends have been wiped out already?" said Reverend Gilmore, his own tequila untouched on the bar in front of him.

El Gato calmly replied, "That insignificant Protestant mission was never in any great danger. Is high in the mountains as our friend here says, and its small congregation consists of unimportant *pobrecitos* who have little to steal and present no danger to our peerless leader, El President Diaz. As my own cell of La Causa puts it together, a small faction of the long-established missionaries there recently had some sort of revelation they were all about to be arrested by *los rurales.* I don't know who could have told them. But I can see why they were most terrified. So they wired north to beg for help. I told you we have our own people strung out along the telegraph lines. That is for how we knew you were coming for to rescue them."

He signaled the barkeep for another round and continued. "Before you and these friends of yours could have left El Paso the frightened quartet at that mission—two women, plus two men who seem to have been on most friendly terms for missionaries—how you say, lit out on their own with four Mexicans for to act as guides and servants. Was a good thing for them they did so. Riding for to meet, they got as far as Ciudad Guerrero, so close and yet so far from here, eh?"

Longarm had finished his own tequila. So he picked up the preacher's as he soberly said, "Good grief. We were planning to steer clear of that garrison town! You say the ones yelling for help are there? What about the others, off to the south?"

El Gato shrugged and replied, "What about them? Do you think either we or the government care two *mierditas* about a handful of *pobrecitos chingados*? They don't need no rescue. They never needed no rescue. Was those who made it to Ciudad Guerrero who need for to be rescued. The were picked up by *los rurales*. Would be a chance for them if they had been arrested by *los federales*. They are not being held as prisoners of war. They are being held by so-called police on the charge of *sospecha*!"

The barkeep had spread five more shot glasses along the bar. Longarm picked up the preacher's second tequila. He felt he needed it as he brought his Cherokee pals up to date. "*Mierditas* are just little balls of shit and he don't think anyone on either side cares about *pobrecitos chingados* or poor fucks. But some of them riding to meet us got picked up on a blanket charge of suspicion, which is all it takes for *los rurales* to do most anything they want to you."

Turning back to El Gato, he asked, "You say there were two Cherokee *gals* riding with them two sissy boys?"

El Gato replied, "Not to worry. We got to *las mujeres* first. I told you was a good thing for them they were riding with sensible Mexican Indians. The two men were picked up in the central marketplace, trying for to buy more trail supplies after riding nearly two hundred of your miles. A servant with them, carrying a basket and wearing no shoes, simply faded into the gathering crowd and ran back to their *posada* for to warn the two *mujeres*. Another servant at the *posada* had friends of friends of La Revolución and thought to send word to us. We got half the party and all their riding stock out of there before *los rurales* made the two men tell them where they had been staying. Knowing *los rurales* as I do, I must say those missionaries were very much in love, or very tough hombres in the end, in spite of the way they had been rattled by mere rumors, along the Rio Verde."

Reverend Gibson gasped, "Lord have mercy, how are we ever going to save those poor boys?"

El Gato downed his own tequila and replied, soberly as ever, "You won't be able to save them. We can bring their frightened companions and fairly valuable saddle and pack mules out here for to join you. Would be one big mistake for another party of *norteamericanos* to ride into Ciudad Guerrero for a time."

Todd Scraper, the older of the two Cherokee riders tagging along, decreed, "*Somebody* has to ride in. Somebody has to try and save those poor boys!"

El Gato shot him a disgusted look and demanded, "Who did you think I ride at the head of, a herd of sheep? Listen, *pendejo mio*, if it was possible for to rescue prisoners from *los rurales* without us getting them killed, we would do so often. As we speak they are holding half a dozen of our closer friends on that same blanket charge of *sospecha*. At such times is best for to cross the fingers and just, how you say, sit in your tights? Is an outside chance they may let those harmless missionaries go. If you try for to take them away from *los rurales,* no *rurale* is going to give you his toys until he has finished *playing* with them, *comprende*?"

Longarm horned in. "Tell you what, gents. Suppose we let our Mex pals smuggle them two missionary gals out here to us tonight and meanwhile I'll mosey on over and pussyfoot around a mite."

El Gato laughed wildly and exclaimed, "You will mosey over? Is thirty of your gringo miles, or a day's cavalry march, and the *chingado* sun would be up before you could get there on my best horse! I sent word for to bring those women and their baggage to you as soon as I knew it was you who'd camped just outside of this village. My friend should have them here for you before noon *mañana*. Would be best for you all to stay here no longer than that and run for the border with half a loaf, instead of staking your lives in a game of all or nothing at all, no?"

Longarm said, "Yes and no. There's more than one way to skin a cat or fuck a *rurale*. So here's my plan."

He turned to the Cherokee preacher to say, "This village is a rebel stronghold. So you and the others will be free to stock up on all the supplies you want whilst you wait here overnight for our rebel pals to bring them missionary gals and their own stock to join you. They ought to be worn to a frazzle when they get here. So you'll want to give 'em the rest of the day to rest up. Meanwhile, you'd best remount 'em on fresh stock you'll have no trouble buying here cheap. *Cheaper* if you throw in their spent mules to sweeten the pot."

"And where will you be all this time?" asked Todd Scraper.

Longarm said, "Going and coming to and from Ciudad Guerrero, with or without them missionary boys. I don't want you all waiting for me. If they capture me I'll try to hold out as long as I can, but we may as well leave your exact route back an open question. That way you won't have to worry about whether I talked or not, see?"

Reverend Gibson said, "That'll be the day! Do you expect us to make it back to the border along some alternate route you never guided us along to begin with?"

Longarm nodded at El Gato and said, "The same Mex rebels who bring them gals out ought to be able to smuggle you north as smart as I was able to smuggle you south. Ain't that right, El Gato?"

The handsome but sinister Mex said, "I shall leave word for them to get your friends back across the Rio Bravo, or die trying. When are we leaving for Ciudad Gurrero, you damned fool?"

Longarm said, "I was planning on leaving directly. I was hoping you'd stay here and see everyone safely on their way about this time tomorrow."

El Gato snorted. "The master of the hacienda does not

gather eggs or milk the cows. I told you I would leave word. Must you have all the fun? You left me behind for to read about it in the papers when you pirated that *federale* gunboat over on the Sea of Cortez."

So that was the way they worked things out, with El Gato seeing the Reverend Gibson got a good buy on canned Mexican grub and somehow finding two handsome black ponies for Longarm and himself in the tricky sunset light.

Longarm told his Cherokee pals he'd catch up with them later, and then he and his Mexican pal were riding through the night to the southwest.

The moonlit trail to Ciudad Guerrero wound *more* than thirty miles, mostly uphill, but El Gato said he liked round numbers.

A railroad train could have covered the distance in an hour. That was the main reason railroad trains were starting to replace horsepower. One cavalryman, on one cavalry mount, could manage thirty miles in twelve hours, resting his mount ten minutes out of every hour and not riding it into the ground by asking it to go all out for any mileage worth mentioning. Stagecoaches and Pony Express riders made far better time, averaging nine miles an hour over hill and dale because they changed horses every ten to fifteen miles. When you subtracted the rest stops of a cavalry column, it averaged three miles an hour.

Drovers herding cattle moved slower, making no more than twelve miles a day on most drives. A man on foot moved across country a tad faster than route-marching cavalry, and that was how come most army regiments across the world of iron and steam were still infantry.

Cavalry and horse-drawn field artillery moved faster, much faster, across your average sized battlefield. That was the only point in having any war horses at all. But despite all the poems about highwaymen at midnight, the only real advantage to riding instead of just walking to

Ciudad Guerrero was that they got to sit down along the way.

They made a little better time than cavalry or even infantry might have when El Gato reined in at a certain rancho along the way to swap ponies. They rode on, and got to swap ponies some more when they met up with those two missionary gals about halfway to Ciudad Guerrero at yet another rancho whose owners knew what was good for them.

Longarm was in a hurry, but took the time to question the scared-looking Cherokee gals about their recent misadventures. They turned out to be twin sisters, Patricia and Gloria Fullbasket. They allowed their friends called them Patty and Glory. They said the two boys they had ridden north with, Pete Redbird and Dick Mayes, knew more than they did about what was going on around their mission. They'd just lit out with the boys because they suspected it would be smart not to stay.

Meanwhile El Gato had questioned the Indian converts riding with the young gals, and as he and Longarm rode on, he confided, "There is no hope. Those two Cherokee they picked up made a terrible mistake before they ever left the marketplace with *los rurales*. They told the *cabrones estupidos* the *truth*! They said they were Protestant Indian missionaries who only wished for to get out of Mexico because they had heard there might be a revolution!"

Longarm asked, "Is that stale news supposed to be some sort of a state secret, for Gawd's sake?"

El Gato explained, "Of course it is supposed to be kept secret. El Presidente with his *mestizo* face covered with pink powder is courting foreign investors with a ferocious erection because he has already fucked Mexico out of all the tax money on tap! When you are a strongman who rules by strength alone, you do not tax the strong who support you. You tax the little people, who have little for to give you, or you tax rich foreigners doing business where they hope for the sweet deals, not the sour taste of losses. So El Presidente does not wish it known that all is not sweetness and light down here, and when people ride for the border bearing such tidings, he does not wish for them to ever leave Mexico alive."

# Chapter 18

Thanks to changing horses twice along the way, they'd made better time than cavalry could have. So though cocks were crowing to either side as they rode into the outskirts of Ciudad Guerrero, it was still fairly dark as El Gato led the way through a maze of back alleyways. It was easy to get lost in Spanish-speaking towns because they built town houses inside out, by Anglo standards. Most of the doors, windows, and veranda railings faced private patios, luxurious or squalid as the family fortunes dictated. So you couldn't tell whether you were in a poor quarter of a Mexican town or riding past the blank stucco walls of the richer folks. Spanish-speaking folks thought it was dumb to let passersby know whether you were worth robbing or not.

When they reined into a lush patio furnished with ole-anders growing around a tiled Moorish fountain, Longarm never asked if the place was owned by kith or kin of El Gato. They said El Gato didn't like to talk about the life he'd led before a *mulatto* named Diaz had given up sucking cocks for a living to steal La Revolución won by the late Benito Juarez.

Turning the ponies over to the household help, El Gato held court in the kitchen as they both coffed up, and

143

when a more ragged rebel told them *los rurales* had just shot their own pals at dawn, but seemed to be holding those missionaries until they received permission from Ciudad Mejico, El Gato proceeded to issue rapid-fire orders Longarm hoped he wasn't really serious about.

Half an hour later, Longarm saw how serious El Gato could be, and what they were doing in such a fancy part of town, when the slender pale-faced Mexican in black cocked his head at the sound of a whistle out back and announced, "*Bueno,* my first commands have been carried out and done well. *Vamos a ver.*"

So they did. They followed a twisted alley on foot to enter the rear of a smaller but richly furnished house that looked as if a herd of buffalo had stampeded through it, with pictures ripped from the stucco walls and drapes hanging everywhere but where they'd first been hung.

In a front parlor they found a bunch of jovial rebels holding a man, a woman, and two terrified kids, a boy of about nine and a girl of mayhaps twelve. The man of the house was in *rurale* uniform. Sort of. His shirt was torn, his lip was split, and he had one boot on and one boot off as he sat in a straight-back chair with his wife seated at his feet on the floor tiles in her nightgown. You could see the kids had been hauled out of bed in their pajamas too. Well-to-do Mexican kids got to sleep late in pajamas. That didn't seem to have gone down too well with El Gato's rebel followers.

The *rurale* officer looked up hopefully when he saw two newcomers with at least as much white blood as his own. He asked what on earth they wanted with poor but honest people.

El Gato said, "I want you to listen to me very carefully, you poor excuse for a person. You are going to tidy up and report to your office a bit late this morning. Should anyone ask for why your face is bleeding, you will tell them your *mujer* beats you."

The *rurale* officer didn't think that was funny. He said,

"How can I report to my office? This is my day off!"

El Gato said, "Of course it is your day off, *mi capitán*. We knew it was your day off. How else would we have found you home with your family instead of torturing our friends at *la cárcel*."

"Listen, I am only forced for to follow orders!" the *rurale* declared.

El Gato's voice was as cold as a well-digger's socks as he replied, "When you get to *la cárcel* you will give orders of your own. We chose you to relay them because we know you outrank the officer of the day. You will bring those two *americano* missionaries back here with you and you alone. If they have not been harmed and you do not try any *pendejo* tricks, you and your family will be released unharmed in return."

The officer protested, "I can only try. But I can't promise you I can do as you ask."

El Gato quietly answered, "One can only do what one can. Let me tell you what I can do to your family if you cannot do what I wish for you to do."

The woman sobbed. "Roberto! For the love of God!"

El Gato hushed her and continued. "The two women shall of course be raped before we kill them, slowly. I do not go in for that sort of thing myself, but I am sure at least a few of my *muchachos* have often wondered what it would be like for to use a *chulo rico* such as your son for a *puta*, eh?"

The rich kid wailed, "*Pero no!* I am not a *mariposa*! Tell them I am not like so, Papa!"

El Gato said, firmly but not emotionally, "We waste time we may not have for to work with. Get cleaned up and move your *culo* if you wish for to ever see any of them alive again!"

So in no time at all the *rurale* officer was out of there, with two of the rebels shadowing him. El Gato said, "*Bueno*. Now we return to the other *casa* with these hostages."

"Do you expect him to double-cross us?" Longarm asked.

El Gato replied, "Don't you? Is an outside chance he wishes for to risk his own skin for his family. Perhaps one in a hundred riding for Diaz has human feelings. In any event, let us all be on our way before this place is surrounded or shelled by field artillery."

Longarm noticed the hard-looking Mexican rebels allowed the two females time to fix their hair as well as get dressed and one scar-faced full-blooded *indio* comforted the frightened boy with a reassuring pat on the back as they were leaving. But he didn't say anything. He knew many Mexicans would rather be called thieving cocksucking bastards than soft.

The hostages were blindfolded in their own patio, and led through back alleyways to that first hideout in the same neighborhood. Since no two patio fountains looked exactly alike, they were marched into an empty adobe walled pantry off the alley entrance, where chairs, a table, and of course some refreshments were carried into them from the nearby kitchen.

El Gato suggested Longarm wait with him in the patio, where they could smoke in the shade of the oleanders while they waited. El Gato said it depressed him to spend much time with people he was going to have executed.

Longarm just reached for one cheroot, knowing the outlaw born and raised a Spanish grandee preferred his own Havana claro brand. As they lit up, Longarm softly asked, "You don't really aim to let any of your *muchachos* rape them *kids,* do you?"

El Gato replied, "Of course not. Do you take me for a barbarian? I only said that to frighten that murderous captain. *When,* not *if,* the treacherous *tiro chingado* crosses us double, we shall merely kill them painlessly and make sure their bodies are never found. Is enough when a man merely has to, how you say, *imagine* his whole fam-

146

ily being tortured and dishonored for who knows how long, eh?"

Longarm started to make a dumb request. But puffing his cheroot in the rational calm of a distinctly Mexican patio, he reflected on what *los rurales* had done for certain to other women and children, and as soon as he had, he had to grudgingly conceded El Gato was a good sport, by the standards of Mexican political dissent.

A pretty, young *chica* came out to serve them from a tray of tapas, or tasty surprises wrapped in pastry envelopes. She poured them tall glasses of *cerveza* to rinse them down, and Longarm was glad when he bit into one tapa stuffed with salty sardine paste and another one filled with either molten lava or those Christ-awful green peppers nobody but a born Mexican could abide.

As he washed away the fire with a milder tapa and plenty of suds, he suspected Mexicans just pickled those little green devils to show off. But he didn't say so. Mexicans laughed when an Anglo blanched at a worm in his tequila, or a gracious offer of iguana lizard baked in bittersweet chocolate.

They'd run out of refreshments and commenced smoking some more when there came a clamor out back, and then more of El Gato's pals led two worn-out and frightened-looking white men in to join them. They *looked* to be white men leastways. But they said they were the Cherokee from that mission, Pete Redbird and Dick Mayes.

El Gato was chattering in Spanish too rapid for Longarm to follow as his own pals brought him up to date. He finally said, *"Bueno,"* then turned to Longarm and declared, "These *hombres* say our gallant captain did not seem to have anyone following him when he came back to his own place alone, with our friends here."

Longarm said, "He must have figured you meant what you said you'd do to his family. How soon can these old boys and me light out, so's you can turn that poor woman and her scared kids loose?"

El Gato said, "Would be suicide for the three of you to make your break before dark. They have not for to know which way you mean for to go. But they will be watching every *camino*. Better we let them search the town for you and, of course, these hostages. They are less likely to shell a *barrio* before they search it if they have some of their own for to worry about, eh?"

Longarm frowned thoughtfully and indicated the two Cherokee as he said, "The farther those others get from us, the harder it's going to be for us to catch up."

El Gato replied, "When darkness falls we shall send you after them with a guide who could trail a black cat through a coal mine on a dark winter's night. I wish I could ride with you. You always seem to have so much fun. But I have been waiting here for others to join me in a, how you say, big push?"

He glanced at the freed missionaries and added, "These *muchachos* look as if they could do with a few hours sleep in any case."

Longarm nodded, and asked Pete Redbird if they'd been tortured or just deprived of food and rest.

The Cherokee said they'd been tossed in an unfurnished cell and left alone, worried too stiff to get much sleep on the stone floor, with their stomachs so knotted they hadn't noticed they were hungry until just recently.

The younger and more Indian-looking Dick Mayes went on to explain how, just before they'd been led to freedom by that one officer, the guards had treated them to shaves and shower baths along with a right hearty breakfast and a whole lot of friendly slaps on their backs.

Neither Longarm nor El Gato commented. They'd both spent nights in Mexican jails.

Longarm said, "I know you boys feel weary, now that you're out of that cell and full of warm grub. But I'm still a tad confounded about the others back at your mission on the Rio Verde. Who was it wired for help and how come most of the others have stayed put if things were getting all that tense down yonder?"

Pete Redbird said *he'd* sent to their co-congregationalists on the Cherokee reserve for help. He explained, "Our mission head, Reverend Squirreltail, seems to hunger for sainthood as a Christian martyr. If I told him once I told him a hundred times that our converts were sure we were all going to be murdered in our beds by their pagan cousins!"

El Gato mused aloud, "Pagans? That far south in the Sierras? Perhaps is possible. The purebloods of Oaxaca, further south, only give lip service to the *santa fe* because they enjoy religious holidays."

Longarm hushed him with a frown and said, "Whether the threat was serious or not is moot. My job was to lead the relief expedition, and I reckon I done it enough if there's nobody else down yonder who's in need of rescue."

Pete Redbird insisted they needed to be rescued. They just didn't know it yet. But Longarm insisted. "They never sent us to drag folks back against their will, kicking and protesting."

Dick Mayes suddenly shook himself like a water spaniel, and Longarm said, "We'd best put you boys to bed lest you fall out of your chairs. We'll have plenty of time on the trail to decide whether this was all a false alarm or not."

El Gato clapped his hands and issued more rapid-fire orders. Some other gals materialized from the oleanders to lead the two missionary boys into the house and put them to bed. It was up to Redbird and Mayes if they wanted any company yonder.

Longarm and El Gato went on jawing in the patio. The black-clad rebel leader told Longarm he meant to fix them up with one of his best trail hands, raised on horseback off a Sierra rancho seized by the Diaz regime for political

pals. El Gato pointed out, and Longarm agreed, that he
and the two young missionaries, riding light with a crack
guide who could question other backers of La Causa along
the way, should have no trouble catching up with the others before their own guides had led them close enough to
the border to require Longarm's multiple skills as a guide,
gunfighter, and all-around tricky cuss.

That pretty *chica* was serving them some more grub in
the shade of an overhead veranda, the sun having chased
them away from the fountain, when they heard the distant
crump of what sounded like a four-pounder.

El Gato answered Longarm's silent question with:
"Noonday gun. The commandante at the *federale* barracks
thinks he's a British officer in some *chingado* colony. Perhaps from his point of view he is. At any rate, he wants
us to know is twelve P.M., and he has modern artillery for
to throw at us. I know what you are thinking. We can't."

Another maid came out of the house to whisper in El
Gato's ear. So the black-clad rebel leader leaped to his
feet, shouting, *"¡Ay, Dios mio, qué pendejada!"* as he ran
into the house with her.

Longarm ran after them, to wind up in a ground-floor
bedroom, where Pete Redbird hung half out of bed, eyes
staring and mouth opened wide in a silent scream, while
young Dick Mayes had rolled out of his bed completely,
to lay spread-eagled on the floor tiles, staring at the rafters
through a mask of vomit.

El Gato's voice hissed like steel being drawn from a
scabbard as he quietly asked, "Do you see why we admire
those venomous spiders so much? They thought you and
these *pobrecitos* would be farther away when the slow
poison they had for breakfast hit. They thought I would
have released those hostages before we knew we had been
crossed double."

Longarm didn't like the look on El Gato's usually prettier face as he coldly added, "They thought wrong, and
you heard me warn that son of a three-legged whore what

would happen to his family if he tried any of their usual tricks!"

Longarm soberly said, "I did. I'm afraid I can't let you carry your threat out, *amigo mio.*"

It got very quiet for a long time before El Gato almost purred at him, "Do my ears deceive me or did I just hear you say you might try for to stop me?"

To which Longarm could only reply, "That's about the size of it."

# Chapter 19

He could see El Gato was in no great hurry to draw, seeing he had plenty of time and knew nobody who beat him to the draw was going to walk out of there alive. So in the time he had to work with, Longarm said, "I know how you feel about the treacherous sons of bitches. It's a natural feeling and we're hardly the first who ever felt it."

He reached for a fresh cheroot as he continued. "The ancient Romans took it out on the innocent kith and kin of guilty parties. So I read this pathetical account by an ancient Roman about this bitty six-year-old girl-child being led to her crucifixion along with her dear old dad, and how even the Roman soldiers wept to hear her asking her daddy what she'd done wrong."

He lit his cheroot and shook out the match as he said, "We know what happened to Ancient Rome. If you ever expect to get a decent Mex republic going, you're going to have to cut the bloodshed, followed by counter-revenge against innocents, down to reasonable."

El Gato snapped, "You heard me give that *rurale chingado* my word, and don't you wish for to pay him back for poisoning these friends of yours?"

Longarm nodded and said, "I do. I want to pay *him* back. I don't have anything against his scared wife and kids. He'd be in deep shit if his clever prank with slow poison got a heap of other men in that same uniform killed, wouldn't he?"

El Gato shrugged and said, "El Presidente does not allow his men to make mistakes. Perhaps that is for why they are so quick on the trigger."

Longarm said, "*Bueno*. Have you got, say, a keg of gunpowder you can spare?"

El Gato replied, "Does a dog have fleas? Most of our own guns are old muzzle-loaders."

Longarm said, "We might be able to issue them new repeating rifles if things work out really well. Let's see about having these bodies tidied up and buried Christian whilst I tell you how I'd really like to get back at them *rurales*."

So he did, and later in La Siesta, which of course had commenced with the firing of that noonday gun atop the fortified barracks of *los federales* on one side of the main plaza, the commandante's blow job was rudely interrupted by a thunderous explosion and the tinkles of cascading window glass outside.

Pushing his young sergeant major's head aside, the portly officer hauled on his pants and grabbed his saber to dash out on the rampart and demand some damned answers!

The fully dressed officer of the day ran up to him to salute and say, "We seem to be under unfriendly fire, *mi corenel*!"

"I can see that!" his superior snapped, adding, *"Guardarte!"* as another bean can filled with black powder and nails exploded with a big white puff in the courtyard below.

A distant voice from their watchtower shouted, "I spotted that one coming in, *mi corenel*! It twinkled in the sunlight, going up as well as arching over and down! It came from the direction of that *rurale* post to our south!"

As if to prove the point, a third missile came whirring

153

in as it tumbled through the sky, and the commandante was dancing in a circle like a fat Comanche war chief as he lost more window glass and one of his troopers screamed in pain down below.

He snarled, "I saw where that one came from! Some *hijos de putas* have no sense of proportion. That low-born *cabrero* they thought they could promote to a policeman is still angry about my innocent little remark to his *mestizo* mistress, is he? *Bueno*. Let us return his fire with our full battery and see how they like *that!*"

The officer of the day, who'd made second lieutenant the hard way instead of by way of political pull, naturally asked if they were sure they were being shelled from the nearby *rurale* post. The thoroughly outraged *federale* C.O. roared, "Who *else* could be shelling us, the *chingado* civilians we allow no repeating *rifles* to? Didn't you just hear me say the greasy halfbreed commanding those other unwashed *cabrones* is a *pendejo* with a pretty mistress and no sense of proportion? I want that field mortar he is using on us silenced and I order this as of five minutes ago!"

So in less than five minutes a full battery of British breech-loading four pounders was merrily reducing the a-dobe-walled *rurale* post to rubble, as if to prove Queen Victoria's munitions makers had known what they were talking about when they'd proposed their four-pound field gun as the vanguard of her expanding colonial empire.

Four pounds of shell casings, shrapnel, and gun-cotton did a hell of lot more damage than a bean can packed with black powder and nails, lobbed clean *over* the *rurale* post from an improvised mortar of sewer pipe wrapped in rawhide. So, as more than one real arillery shell flew over its intended target, El Gato laughed and told Longarm it was time they hauled ass from the alleyway they'd been firing from.

Longarm grinned back, but said, "We'd best take our

154

*battery* with us, lest they ever figure out how we did that just now!"

El Gato snapped orders to the four rebels with them, and the six of them lit out through the twisting maze of back alleyways with their improvised mortar and a couple of "shells" they hadn't been able to send off before the outraged *federales* had proceeded to bombard that whole neighborhood.

The rebels could always use the cans left as hurled grenades, and real shells were still raining down in the distance as they made it back to that patio filled with oleanders.

When Longarm marveled how the shelling had gone on for so long, El Gato chortled, "I know. Is it not marvelous? By this time someone from *los rurales* should have managed a cease-fire. But one does not wave a truce flag from atop a mound of debris if one is dead. So I forgive you for saying I should not kill that treacherous captain's wife and children. I don't even wish for to fuck the wild-eyed woman or her skinny daughter. I owe them no favors. But after I know you and your guide are safely on your way, I shall let those hostages go. Perhaps the government will execute the wife of such a *pendejo*. Is not for me to worry about. Thanks to you we have made those suckers of cock in Ciudad Mejico most confused, and no doubt very, how you say, pissing in their mother's milk?"

Longarm laughed and said, "Nope, *you* gents say that. We say pissed off. Meanwhile, seeing we must have everyone on the other side mighty mixed up right now, I'd like to chance a run for it this side of sundown. I have some catching up to do, and the advantage of owlhoot riding evens out a mite when you consider they'll have had more time to *think* by the time the night birds sing."

El Gato didn't think much of the notion. But as Longarm pointed out, a man notorious for his night vision had a more natural hanker for darkness than natural folks on either side.

So Longarm and the rebel guide assigned to him rode out on fresh mounts within the hour, with the sun on high but the air filled with dust and most everybody in town over by the main plaza to marvel at the scene of total chaos.

El Gato had promised to turn those hostages loose after sundown, and Longarm figured he was just as likely to keep his word to a friend as he was to an enemy. So he put that problem behind him, and there was no way he could talk to his Mexican rebel guide about those two poisoned Cherokee, even if she'd been a boy.

The rancher's daughter El Gato had detailed to lead Longarm after those others had more white blood than that maid at the Eagle Hotel, but less than most of the so-called Cherokee he'd been riding with. There was no financial advantage to being Indian or part Indian down Mexico way. So he knew she'd be pissed if anyone hinted she wasn't a member of the Sangre Azul landed class, even though the dictatorship currently in office had taken her family's land away.

She'd been introduced to him as Lucia, followed by a whole string of names that doubtless impressed Mexicans a bit more. Her English was better than his Spanish, and she said she didn't mind when he asked if he could call her Lucy.

He didn't ask, but figured she was in her middle twenties, with cameo features that could have gotten her courted seriously in London or New York despite her olive complexion, blue-black hair, and eyes the greenish black of a champagne bottle, an *expensive* champagne bottle. She was dressed like a male *vaquero* in dark leather trimmed with coin-silver conches. Her cordovan-brown sombrero looked as if it might fly away with her in a stiff wind. She had it tied on good with a braided leather chin strap.

She agreed they'd stand as good a chance on a confused afternoon as they might in a thoughtful night. So they rode for it with the sun low behind them, and chased their shadows down to the desert to the east without a hint of pursuit by the time the moon rose to show the way. Longarm noticed they stopped twice in the night for fresh mounts, although not at the same spreads he and El Gato had stopped at, riding the other way. Making even better time, they circled Bachiniva in the tricky light of dawn to breakfast and swap ponies at a secluded *ranchita* surrounded by pear flats at the base of the Sierra de las Tunas.

Longarm understood why when the ranch folks there, who seemed to be kissing kin to Lucy from the way they acted, told them the other Mexican guiding the larger Cherokee bunch had decided to follow the desert trail leading to Santa Clara, *east* of the Sierra de las Tunas, in case *los rurales* or *los federales* had heard they'd traveled south along the cooler cactus-covered ridges.

Lucy agreed with Longarm that if the other side had any line at all on the relief expedition, they'd have heard by now that they weren't following the same route back. Meanwhile, along the crests of the Sierra de las Tunas was a faster way back than they figured to find on the hot desert floor as that other desert stream ran ever downward into those infernally soggy bottomlands.

Lucy said the other Mexican guide would be smarter than that. She figured he'd follow the Santa Clara to where it joined forces and rounded a big bend south of Villa Ahumada, after which, if the Cherokee got over an unmapped desert pass she knew of, they'd be just about home free for a hard day's ride for the border.

When Longarm asked where the handiest crossing might be that far downstream from El Paso, Lucy told him, "For Mexicans in no trouble with the government, Bosque Benito. If I was a gringa being chased by *rurales chingados*, I would, how you say, pussyfoot upstream for to cross at your Fort Hancock, a little upstream from Mexican Customs at El Porvenir."

So Longarm allowed that was the place to head, hoping to catch up with the others to offer such help as they might need.

Coffeed, grubbed, and mounted on fresh ponies they'd have to take better care of for a spell, they lit out for the shady western slope of the Sierra de las Tunas, meaning to make some time before they and their fresh mounts ran out of steam.

He noted with approval that for such a delicate-featured little gal, Lucy rode tough as any hombre her *vaquero* outfit might have been intended for to begin with.

When he said so, during a trail break, sharing Mexican canned beans, Lucy shrugged, looked away, and softly said, "Was my, how you say, kid brother's *traje charro*. *One* of them, I mean to say. He was wearing other clothes the day *los rurales* shot him and my husband."

Longarm allowed he was sorry held asked. She smiled defiantly and added, "They did not die against any fucking *wall*! They both went down fighting, *muy hombre*, and they died not alone that day. They took six of the *hijos de las putas* with them!"

Longarm gravely replied, "You were right. They went down like men."

The pretty Mexican widow woman finished her beans, belched delicately, and said, "I try for to pay the government back every chance I get. I have killed more of them than my brave men were able to. They were ambushed. I try to avoid riding into their traps. It gets easier as one practices the games we play. That trick you played on them back in Ciudad Guerrero was a new one, and I laughed until I cried when I heard how you'd gotten those *chingados* for to kill one another. I had of course heard tales of El Brazo Largo. But to tell the truth, I have not believed some of them."

Longarm warned himself sternly not to take her up on those eyelash flutters before they'd caught up with the others.

So he behaved and she behaved when they reined in atop the ridge to fashion yet more cactus shelters along about noon. They were both worn down and it was too hot, even up yonder, to think of anything more strenuous than sleep.

So they slept until around four P.M., and rode on along the ridge trail until sundown, when they agreed it would be risky to ride on in the dark over such uncertain footing.

So this time, when they made camp and took more time with their canned suppers, she seemed to feel it was only natural to tag along when Longarm allowed they'd had a long day, there was a chill in the air now, and it might be a good notion to try for a night's sleep for a change.

He'd meant it. His heart had been pure, or reasonably pure, as he sat on his bedding in another cactus cave, shucking his boots. But all his virtuous notions seemed to just take wing as pretty little Lucy peeled off her *vaquero* duds as if they were old pals, then calmly joined him, naked as a jay and built far better, atop his bedroll.

In less time than it takes to tell about it, they really *had* become old pals.

Or damned good pals leastways.

For it was hard not to like a wiry little gal with tits a size large for her petite frame when she got on top, in high-heeled boots with spurs, to slide up and down your raving erection like a wooden pony on a merry-go-round pole, laughing like a kid really enjoying a swell new ride at the county fair.

# Chapter 20

The next few days, riding alone with Lucy, could be summed up as mighty exciting. Mighty tense and exciting on the trail, and mighty nice and exciting most of the other time, save for a stolen moment hither or yon to eat, sleep, or heed other calls of nature.

Like El Gato himself, Lucy, as Lucia, considered herself Sangre Azul because her family had possessed a lot of land and at least some Spanish blood. But unlike El Gato, who was a natural man and, like all natural men from emperors down, democratic when it came to fornication, Lucy had perforce been more particular about who she'd coupled with as the daughter of a *ranchero grande* and the widow of a hero of La Revolución. So, in sum, she hadn't been getting any lately, and as a once happily married woman, she really knew how to screw and really liked to. She confided on their second session in another clump of cactus that as long as they were never likely to meet again, she had a few naughty notions she'd never dared mention to the very few Mexican rebels worthy of her favors.

So Longarm got to brush up on dirty Spanish as they got to know each other better, in the biblical sense. He'd already known most Mexican gals used the poetical "*el rapto supremo"* for coming, and that *"chupar"* was to suck, while *"comer,"* despite what it sounded like, was to eat. But *"tragosas"* for a blow job was less familiar to him, although sort of poetical when you considered it meant "that which is swallowed."

They even got to *talk* to one another some of the time. He'd brought his sensuous guide up to date on his mission so far, or up to date as far as he could understand it. Lucy agreed, snuggled in the bedroll they were sharing under a desert moon, that both those false-alarm messages from Rio Verde and that fatal dash for the faraway border by no more than four of those Cherokee missionaries made no sense.

But Pete Redbird, who'd confessed to sending those wires, and Dick Mayes, who'd gone along with him, were in no shape to explain, thanks to that slow poison they'd had for breakfast.

There was no way to wire their mission and compare notes, and whether the Cherokee twin sisters who'd ridden off with them knew whether the late Pete Redbird had been up to something or not, they were out in the lead with the main rescue party. So farther along, as the old church song went, he'd likely know more about it.

Meanwhile, as the same church song advised, they walked, rode, or made love in the sunshine, assured they'd know more about it farther along.

Lucy led him down off the cover along the Sierra de las Tunas for a moonlight ride, punctuated by a day hiding out in a timbered draw bare-ass, and then up a lower cactus-covered fault block and through a pass that wasn't on any survey map. They camped the next day on the cooler eastward-facing slope, and even though he'd already noticed, he let Lucy point out the fresh horse apples and the refilled slit trench where somebody had buried their own shit. Young gals took such delight in showing a man messy sights they thought he'd never seen up until he'd met them.

Unlike hound dogs and rattlesnakes, good human trackers didn't have to follow the spoor of any man or beast they were tracking over hill and dale and around every turn. That "sixth sense" Eastern dudes were inclined to hang on Western trackers, Anglo, Indian, or Mexican, came from having the common sense to foresee, or make an educated guess, which way those being tracked had gone once you'd cut their sign near a fork in the road.

So Longarm didn't ask why when Lucy pointed east-northeast to say that the main party would be holed up for the rest of the day in a village just over the horizon. But she explained, "I know this Juanito Chavez who conveyed the twin sisters to your friends and had order for to guide them all safely to the border. He has people in the village of Nueva Santa Monica. Would be most sensible for him to kill the two *pajaros* with one *piedra*. They can hide among villagers *simpatico* to La Causa, and Chavez can determine who might be between them and the Rio Bravo before he leads another moonlight ride, eh?"

Longarm nodded and said, "I follow your drift. If we hunker down in any shade we might find out ahead, they're likely to have moved on by the time we can catch up. So do you reckon riding on in by broad day will be safe, seeing the folks in and about a . . . How come they built a village out here in the middle of nowhere, *querida*?"

She said, "Is a stagecoach stop and a, how you say, telegraph relay station, surrounded by the usual *pobrecitos* it takes for to feed and shovel *mierda* for a handful of government people."

Longarm whistled and said, "Now that you mention it, that does look like a line of telegraph poles on the horizon off to our right. I'd have thought that other rebel, Chavez, should have known that."

Lucy replied, "Of course he did. But one hand, how you say, washes the other when one mans a telegraph relay on the Chihuahua desert. I do not see why any underpaid civil servant would wish for to risk his life, and the lives of his woman and children, when all he has to do is to stay away from that *chingado* telegraph key and answer questions from the outside world later, if they should ever be asked."

So they rode on, and on, as Longarm mulled her calming words over. When she said they weren't headed the right direction, Longarm told her, "Yes, we are. You ride on ahead if it's getting too hot for you. I'll just ride on over to that telegraph line and cut me a wire, out of sight of that village, before we all gather round for that last dash to the border. I just hate it when they wire ahead of me whilst I'm getting there so much slower in the saddle!"

She protested. "Wait! If you cut the telegraph wire, the national service will send a repair crew, with a *federale* guard."

He said, "I sure hope so. I'd rather have any *federales* in this neck of the Chihuahua headed our way on horseback than laying for us over by the border. Ain't you never played *ajedrez* before?"

She laughed, said she was beginning to see why her detested government had posted that bounty on his head, then added she'd always wanted to visit the United States and might as well, seeing she'd never be able to retrace her route to Ciudad Guerrero now.

So they rode over at a walk to avoid raising dust, and Longarm stood on his borrowed stock saddle's broad swells with his hand on the sun-silvered cedar of a telegraph pole to give himself a head start. Then he shinnied the rest of the way up with his all-purpose pocket knife.

Once his head and shoulders were even with the single strand strung across that stretch of the nationalized network, Longarm had a bird's-eye view of the tiny village shimmering in the heat waves off to his northwest and everything closer between. So he shinnied back down a lot faster than he'd shinnied up.

Lucy asked, "What is the matter? For why did you not cut the wire?"

He said, "We ain't alone out here. There's about two dozen dismounted riders and as many ponies, strung out along a dry wash betwixt here and yonder village, fortunately facing the other way. They're covering the village with their saddle guns."

She crossed herself and whispered, "Victorio?"

He shook his head and said, "Mexicans. Dressed too casual to be *los rurales*, and you say most folks in that village they're stalking are in good standing with La Revolución. That leaves plain old bandits. The way I read it, they cut the trail of our Cherokee pals and, not content with the edge they have on ten men and half a dozen women, mean to jump them later this evening as they ride out of town unsuspecting."

Lucy asked, "What can we do but ride away while we still have the chance? There is no help we can reach out to for more than a day's ride in any direction. I know they are your friends. Juanito is my friend. But there is nothing we can do for to help them."

Longarm said, "You're wrong. I could swing around to the far side and ride in to join them churchgoing Cherokee with my own three guns. Making it eleven men to twenty."

Lucy pleaded, "Please don't! I like you too much for to see you die as my brother and husband died, in a brave but futile fight!"

But he said he had to do what he had to do, and she said she had to save her own ass. So they parted on good terms without taking the time for more than a kiss. Then Longarm rode the other way, feeling lonesome as he circled Nueva Santa Monica just over its horizon to mosey on in from the northeast with the distant border to his back, the last direction anyone should have been expecting him from.

He was naturally spotted from the village long before

he reined in out front of the small adobe church and more imposing stagecoach stop and telegraph relay combined. He was met by barking dogs, laughing kids, and most everybody he'd been riding with before.

As he dismounted, a clean-cut young Mexican who had to be Juanito Chavez asked him how he'd avoided those bandits who had them all pinned down.

As the Reverend Gibson, Todd Scraper, and young Jim Whitemark came over, Scraper and Whitemark toting rifles, Longarm chuckled and declared, "I'm pleased as hell to see I ain't the only old soldier with this outfit. They don't have us surrounded. There's only a score of them, waiting for dark, in a wash a quarter mile to the south. How do you reckon you all figured you all for the gold at the end of their rainbow?"

The naturally suspicious Todd Scraper said, "That's easy. They're after the girls, our guns, and our horseflesh, in that order."

Longarm wrinkled his nose and said, "Don't forget your boots. But I ain't so sure. You can see from their cautious approach that they don't have you down as sissies. They only have us outnumbered two to one before we consider how tough any of the *gals* might be. Such odds are seldom risked for low stakes in the bandit game. So they must have heard about that thousand in silver you're still packing, Rev."

The Cherokee preacher sighed and said, "Lord knows plenty of their own kind could have gossiped. For I had to pay in silver, a lot of silver, replenishing our depleted trail supplies and buying some fresh riding stock between here and as far as we ever got, blast that Peter Redbird's bones!"

Longarm replied, "We can ask the Fullbasket twins about all that, once we get us all out of this fix. You didn't fail exactly, and you ought to have most of your expense money left, so . . ."

"What if we offered them the remaining silver dollars,

if that's all they're really after?" the Cherokee preacher asked.

Todd Scraper growled, "Hold on there, sky pilot. That's the *Lord's* money you're talking so freely about!"

The older man snapped back, "No, it isn't! Our rescue operation was funded by our friends from the former Confederacy."

Before the argument could get sillier, Longarm cut in to tell them, "Who them cartwheels belong to is moot. If you offer them the money they'd take it. Then they'd kill you for everything else you had. You don't make deals with Mex bandits. Mex rebels, yes. Mex military men, maybe. *Los rurales*, once in a blue moon when you have no other choice. But bandits? Never."

Young Chavez backed him, morosely muttering, *"Es verdad."*

Longarm turned to him to say, "They're expecting us to ride on after sundown. When they see we haven't, they may give it up, or they may attack under cover of darkness. Do you reckon you could get some of these villagers to help us throw up barricades across all the ways in and out betwixt those adobe walls?"

Chavez said, "It will be done. But won't they know, as soon as we begin, that we must be, how you say, on to them?"

Longarm nodded soberly and replied, "Sure they will. They'll see they have their choice between charging in across an open field of fire in broad daylight or just forgetting the whole fool notion."

So a short time later Chavez had his kith and kin piling baskets and barrels and filling them with loose dirt, to fort up the gaps between the outlying adobe buildings, making them as bullet-proof as those thick walls themselves.

Knowing where the bandits would be observing all this action from, Longarm, his Yellowboy, and smaller arms were supervising the earthworks to the south when the telegraph operator came out of his relay station to ask what was going on.

Longarm said, "Bandits. We'd be much obliged if you didn't put that on your wire, though. There's some things we'd as soon keep to our own selves, if you follow my drift and know what's good for you."

The government man said, "That is another thing I wished for to talk to you about. Did you cut our wire or did they? I can't seem to send or receive at the moment."

Longarm knew *he* hadn't cut the wire. So he said, "It was them, I reckon. They sure seem mighty determined for a band of roving thugs."

As if to prove his point, someone pointed and said, *"Mira, ellos venes."* Sure enough, three gents wearing big sombreros with lots of bullets across their dirty shirts were riding in under a flag of truce, or a white flour sack.

Longarm braced his left shoulder against an adobe wall, and trained his carbine around the corner to call out in Spanish that they'd come close enough.

By this time he'd been joined by the Reverend Gibson and most of the other men. So he said, "Keep your fool heads down. Todd, Jim, and Stretch, I want you to round up some of the others and guard the other approaches whilst I see what these sneaky rascals have to say."

As they faded back, the rider next to the one waving the white flag called out, "Hey, gringo, there is no need for you to die. Just give us all that fifty thousand Yanqui dollars and we will go away, see?"

Longarm called back, "We don't have *one* thousand left. So why don't you go away before you get yourself killed for small change?"

The bandit leader, or spokesman leastways, laughed and called back, "Hey, gringo, you got a sense of humor, eh? I know fifty thousand is a lot of money. But you *cabrónes* are rich and you can always get *more*, eh? You give us the money or you die, *hijos de putas!*"

So Longarm shot him, and seeing it was a repeating

carbine, blew the other two out of their saddles before they could come unstuck.

As their three ponies bolted off in three directions, the Reverend Gibson gasped, "Oh, Dear Lord! You shot those three men out from under a flag of truce!"

Longarm stared poker-faced at the three forms stretched out in the middle distance as the dust settled. "They called my momma a whore," he said, "and where else but under a flag of truce can you take such an easy aim at anybody who's just said right out that they mean to kill you?"

# Chapter 21

The Cherokee preacher and doubtless former Confederate officer went on fussing until Longarm pointed out they wouldn't have cut the telegraph wire and tipped their hand if they hadn't been planning to take the money and run. He said, "We're far enough north now to be in the way of them *federales* patrolling for Victorio. So now we've whittled them bandits down to seventeen or so, with or without their leader. They might wait almost a full day and try for an all-out night attack on us. They might have the brains to light out before we have more company."

Reverend Gibson asked, "Then you think our best choice would be to just sit tight until those Mexican troops ride in?"

Longarm wrinkled his nose and replied, "Not hardly. Not *this* child, at any rate. There's an outside chance *los federales* might just arrest everybody and await further orders from Mexico City. At best you'll be hung up for weeks or more if they decide to let your rich Texican pals go your bail. But they're on the prod, may not feel they have time for games, and just let you all vanish somewhere in Old Mexico, the way a heap of others, including Mexicans, have been known to."

"You don't paint a rosy picture," the Cherokee preacher

said. When he asked if Longarm had any other choices to offer, the laconic lawman said, "Yep. We ride out of here this morning, men on the flanks and gals in the middle, whilst they're still arguing about their own next moves. They'll have us outnumbered and outgunned, but not quite two to one no more, and by now they should have noticed you have at least one serious shootist riding with you. Fighting it out in the open in broad daylight might not suit their fancy. If they do go for broke, that's still not as bad as waiting here like penned sheep for *los federales* to sheer or slaughter, as the spirit moves them. Ain't no way in hell we're going to fight off a whole cavalry platoon, and they never patrol in smaller numbers during an Indian scare!"

So the Cherokee preacher called his pals Scraper and Tiawa together for a powwow, and both former Confederate raiders agreed Longarm's plan was risky as all getout but better than any *they* could come up with.

As the others were getting set to make a run for it, Longarm took young Chavez to one side and said, "As you've doubtless figured by now, we're fixing to bust out wild and woolly and you don't have a dog in this fight. So we'll understand if you'd as soon lay low amid your kith and kin here. Neither bandits, cavalry, nor mounted police are likely to waste time pestering poor folks, no offense."

The young Mexican soberly replied, "I have been wondering what happened to your own guide. I was ordered for to guide this party safely to the Rio Bravo. If I cannot get you there, I will go down fighting on your side. A man can only do his best, and if I fail, nobody will be able to say I ran away like that other *cabrón*!"

Longarm quietly replied, "It wasn't exactly a *he* goat and it was my suggestion, should anyone ever ask. But seeing you seem to be as *loco en la cabeza* as me, I'll be proud to ride and, if need be, fight beside you, hombre!"

So Juanito and his rebel pals among the villagers

rounded them up fresh mounts, broke open a barricade on the side of town farthest from the last *known* location of that outlaw band, and seventeen of them, counting Chavez and the Fullbasket twins, lit out in a column of threes at a mile-eating trot that didn't lift as much dust as a full gallop might have.

Longarm rode right flank, out a furlong toward that wash those other riders had been hiding in. But nothing happened. They'd given up and lit out themselves, or they were having trouble working up the nerve for a showdown at even numbers, though half a dozen of Longarm's party were gals.

But gals toting guns were still gun toters, and having seen what a murderous marksman at least one of the party had proven himself to be, the bandits held off, if they were still there, until Chavez had led the way over the flat horizon and announced, during a rest stop, that they were now less than eighty miles, or two mighty hard nights in the saddle, from the crossing near Fort Hancock.

They still had to get there, of course. So their guide led them off to one side of their beeline to yet another sleepy little desert crossroads where, surprising as it might seem, he had other kith and kin who didn't think much of the current government.

It was becoming ever more obvious why El Gato had chosen Juanito Chavez to guide the main party. Longarm owed El Gato a favor if pretty little Lucia had been chosen for *his* guide with malice aforethought.

They got there just in time for La Siesta. They had no government folks to worry about, and whatever the village was doing in the middle of all that low chaparral, they surely had a lot of horses in many a corral. When Longarm asked if it was some sort of rebel remount depot, Chavez just looked away and murmured, *"Quien sabe?"* So Longarm didn't ask any more questions.

Whoever and whatever the villagers were, they fixed the eleven men and six women up with adjoining ground-floor rooms, the gals sharing two to a room, in what seemed a long, converted stable near one of the corrals. The adobe partitions between chambers were newer than the thicker original walls, and each double Dutch door opened onto the loose baked-brick veranda running from one end to the other. There was a tack room in the middle of the row where they could store their harnesses, saddles, and trail supplies. Most everybody naturally toted their bedrolls, saddlebags, and saddle guns to the rooms they'd chosen to bed down in. Longarm told them to try and catch up on their sleep so they could push at least forty miles as soon as it cooled some.

As others hustled and bustled, Longarm scouted up the brown-haired Alice Bluejacket and asked if he could have a word in private with her. She stepped into the tack room with him, smiling crookedly with one brow arched. He said, "Miss Bluejacket, I've noticed you seem to be in charge of the trail supplies whenever there's occasion to dole any out."

She nodded and said she'd been in charge of church alms back on their reservation. He said, "I thought so. I need your help with them Fullbasket twins. Once everyone settles down, I mean to pay them a visit and see how they feel about a friendly little orgy."

The prim little Cherokee gal blanched and gasped, "And you're asking my help? You dare? What kind of an unfeeling monster are you anyway? Those poor girls have just been through a terrible experience, and for heaven's sake, they're missionaries!"

He nodded soberly and said, "From a mission leastways. They'd have been mere children, the same as Pete Redbird and Dick Mayes, when that mission to remote Tsalagi speakers was established back before the war."

Alices tamped her pretty foot and blazed, "That's no excuse for making improper advances, damn you! You're crazy, crazy, crazy if you think I'd be party to anything so vile and dirty as a sex orgy with twin sisters!"

Longarm said, "I never said I figured on *having* an orgy with 'em. I know they'll think I'm a dirty dog. I want you to do something sneaky whilst the two of them are busy coping with me, see?"

She scowled, said, "I know I shouldn't ask," then said. "Just what on earth are you really after?"

He told her. Her eyes got big as saucers and she started to say no. But when he told her he was either right or wrong, and that either way it was in the interest of her church and nation to find out, she laughed and allowed she'd try.

So Longarm smoked a cheroot under the *ramada* to let things sort of settle down before he moseyed over to the room the Fullbasket twins were sharing, and barged in without knocking to catch them in an act of love that was hardly sisterly. They were both stark naked atop one bedroll in the position Mexicans described *al reverso*. It certainly looked *perverso,* and Longarm knew that some night when he was all alone in his own bedroll, he was going to suffer vivid memories of those two tolerably well-built little things shoving all that hot pussy in each other's faces. So he managed to sound sincere as he shut the double door behind him, plunging everyone back in darkness as he asked if they'd mind if he joined them.

Patricia Fullbasket, or maybe it was Gloria, called him a no-good Peeping Tom, while Gloria, or maybe it was Patricia, told him to peek at his mother's naked ass while he jacked himself off.

He said, "Aw, don't be like that, ladies. Your little secret is safe with *me*. Have either of you ever read that book *Justine* by that poor loon de Sade? Now *there* was an old boy who knew how to combine incest with perversion in spades!"

Then some naked lady was up against him in the dark, flailing at him with her fists while she tried to knee him in the nuts. Another one was hissing like a snake about calling the law on him. So he told them he'd just be on his way if they didn't like boys, and naturally, neither was in any shape to follow him outside.

He moseyed down to the end of the veranda and around the corner to meet Alice Bluejacket there. The Cherokee gal held out a fifty-dollar note to him as she marveled, "They have *bales* of this paper money in the bottoms of their packsaddles, under women's unmentionables and old Bibles printed in Sikwayi's alphabet! But how did you know?"

Longarm shrugged and said, "I didn't expect Cherokee Bibles, albeit I reckon since nobody was reading them, they figured they'd just carry them home atop the paper money they'd stolen. I expected that paper money, or something they'd feel as much call to steal, because I was having a tough time figuring out how those two Cherokee boys got picked up in the central market of a good-sized town, just shopping like other tourists, unless somebody tipped *los rurales* off to them *being* there."

The brown-haired Cherokee gasped, "You mean those twins, waiting for them back at their hotel?"

He said, "*Posada*. They went to a *posada* or wayside inn with their fellow travelers, and contacted rebels their Mexican guides knew *before* they ever tipped off *los rurales*."

The more decently brought-up Cherokee gal started to ask why. Then she nodded soberly and said, "So *that's* the fifty thousand dollars those Mexican bandits somehow heard tell of, and fifty thousand split two ways comes to twice as much as fifty thousand split four ways!"

Longarm said, "The twins seem more fond of one another than I'd say they were of those old boys they lit out with. In fairness to them twins, Redbird and Mayes might have been planning to double-cross *them* once they made it across the border. Nights get lonesome on the trail, but like you just said, two ways is twice as much as four ways."

Alice asked, "What do you mean to do now, arrest them?"

He sighed and replied, "Not down here in Old Mexico. My badge don't cut no ice south of the border. Ain't sure what I can charge them with *north* of the border. But mum's the word and we'll let our own country worry about what's to be done with 'em after we get this whole fool's errand safely back to Texas."

He put the fifty-dollar note she'd given him away, allowing it was evidence. She repressed a shudder and told him he was welcome to such blood money.

So they split up and later on, when the siesta ended and they'd all had a warm set-down early supper, Longarm told them they should all move out before sundown, seeing as nobody was looking, it was much cooler, and they had a long way to go.

They rode through the night and into the break of day a ways before they holed up in a forty-acre pear patch for the day, then rode on half rested for another full night, to ride into another tiny town at dawn, where Chavez said they ought to be safe for the day if they stayed out of sight. They were less than a mile from the Rio Bravo and both sides of the border were being patrolled considerably, thanks to nobody knowing where in thunder Victorio had gone after leaving La Candelaria before any cavalry could get near enough to matter.

This time Longarm bedded down in a hayloft overlooking the door to the storage shed most of their gear, including the packsaddles of the Fullbasket twins, had been stored in.

That was where the Cherokee blonde, Clovinia Spotted Deer, caught up with him. Joining him in the nest he'd hollowed for his bedding in the hay, Clovinia first acted surprised that Alice Bluejacket wasn't up there with him.

Longarm calmly replied, "You knew she wasn't up here with me. Why are you trying to low-rate a straitlaced church secretary who never said anything about your swimming sesssions, even though I suspect she noticed?"

Clovinia flushed. "All right, you've been . . . swimming with somebody else. Do you expect me to believe you've been keeping that love tool I know so well all to your own little hand?"

He shrugged and replied, "Not hardly. Why do you ask? Have you been playing with yourself?"

She sobbed, "Yes, and it's driving me crazy! You know how warm-natured I am, darling! Why have you been avoiding me?"

He smiled thinly and told her, truthfully enough, "I've been sort of busy, and I thought it was your own great notion that we should quit whilst we were ahead."

She smiled sheepishly and confessed, "I was wrong. I want some, I need some, I need it *now*!"

So, lest she think him a sissy, Longarm proceeded to shuck his jeans as she busted more than one button getting undressed. Then they were old pals again. He'd forgotten how nice she moved under a man, and how different it looked sliding in and out as it parted that blond pubic hair, after all those other times with the more wiry Lucy under similar conditions. And then, just as they were trying to come again, all hell seemed to be breaking loose down below as someone clanged on an alarm triangle while women, pigs, and chickens squawked all around.

So Longarm rolled off the Cherokee blonde to haul on his duds, boots, and six-gun before he snatched up his Stetson and Yellowboy to go down the damned ladder and find out what was going on.

What was going on, he saw, as he joined Chavez, the *alcalde,* and the mixed crowd of Mexicans and Cherokee at the gate of the low wall around the tiny trail town, was a mounted platoon of riders dressed in the gray charro outfits and big gray felt sombreros of *los rurales.* And they weren't headed anywhere but directly at those assembled at the one way in or out.

176

Chavez murmured, "The back wall is not too high for to jump."

Longarm sighed and said, "Not on horseback, and how far were any of you planning to outrun those mounted police on foot? Has anybody here got a white kerchief? I'd best go on out and have a talk with the sons of bitches!"

Chavez gasped, *"Pero no, El Brazo Largo!* Have you forgotten that ten-thousand-peso reward on your head?"

To which Longarm could only reply, "How could one forget? But let me do the talking and I might be able to save most of the bunch."

# Chapter 22

The *rurales* reined in to sit their ponies in a long, ragged line when they spotted Longarm coming out to them waving a kerchief. He'd handed his saddle gun to Chavez, but still wore his .44-40. Anyone could see it was a futile gesture, but he didn't want to look like a sissy.

As he got within conversational range, the sergeant in command smiled down at him and remarked, "Nice boots, *señorito*. Has anyone ever told you that you fit the description of that *asesinato El Brazo Largo*? It was just on the wire that he could be headed our way."

To which Longarm calmly replied, "*Muchas gracias.* I've heard about that old boy and they say he's a good-looking white man. Our Bureau of Indian Affairs has me down as a Roger Tenkiller of the Cherokee tribe. We don't rate our own nation no more. Let me show you."

He stepped closer, sticking the kerchief in a hip pocket as he got out his fake B.I.A. allotment card and that fifty-dollar bill.

The sergeant's face was impassive as he saw what he'd been offered. He bent down to take them with his back to most of his men. Whether he read English or not, he went through the motions, then handed the card back, without the paper money. He nodded and said, "Keep talking. I like what you have said so far."

Longarm smiled thinly and replied, "I thought you might. Why don't you get down off your high horse so's we can have a word in private, man to man?"

"How do I know I can trust you not to do anything heroic with that double-action Colt?" asked the *rurale,* adding with a sly grin, "I want *that* too."

Longarm said, "They tell this story about these natives who eat monkeys, catching the monkeys with a handful of peanuts in a hollow gourd."

The sergeant was dismounting as he sullenly replied, "I have heard the story. The monkey sticks his hand through a hole just big enough for him to reach inside for the peanuts. Once he has his fist full he is unable for to get his hand out. Are you trying to warn me not to be greedy? Did you think I joined *los rurales* for to be *generous*?"

Longarm said, "I'm trying to warn you not to be *foolish.* I want you to listen carefully. I have an offer to make that you would be foolish to refuse. I don't expect you to *like* me any more than I like you, but I think I can show you how one hand might wash the other and how we have to trust each other to make it work."

So the sergeant listened, raised a few objections Longarm explained away, and then, while a *rurale* sergeant wasn't about to shake with a gringo, red or white, said, "Is a deal. But remember you have one of your Yanqui miles for to ride to the ferry, and none of you will be able to make it if there are any tricks!"

So Longarm turned around and strode back to the village gate, where he told those assembled, "We've made a deal. Let's commence to saddle up and I'll explain as we go."

Fran Baker, the blue-eyed brunette white girl in the bunch, caught up with him as he was saddling the two ponies Chavez had wrangled for him. She said, "Something odd is going on. I know something odd is going on.

179

You have to tell me what's going on, darn it!"

Longarm said, "I ain't got time and I won't be sure of all my facts until I can send some wires and get some blamed answers, Miss Fran."

He pointed at the open door of the nearby storage shed and added, "We got to get a move on. Before them *rurales* have second thoughts about the offer I just made 'em. Let me get you all safely across the border and you have my word I'll drop by your place in El Paso and tell you all about it before I leave for Denver!"

So they shook on it and she scampered to catch up. Everyone else in the party made short work of loading up their riding and pack ponies. As some commenced to mill, Longarm called out for them to dress column-of-files on young Chavez, seated on his riding mount alone near one corner of the village plaza. Longarm shouted, "Chavez will take the point! I'll bring up the rear as we single-file from here to the Rio Bravo or, have it your way, Rio Grande. Don't nobody stop and don't nobody look back, lest you wind up in a worse fix than Lot's wife in the Good Book."

As first the Reverend Gibson and then Todd Scraper walked their ponies in the right direction, Longarm, still on his feet, stopped the nearest Fullbasket twin and her two ponies, saying, "I'm sorry, Miss Patricia, unless it's Gloria, but you have to leave that pack pony and its load behind."

The Cherokee gal stared down owl-eyed and protested, "I can't leave that packsaddle! I won't give up my unmentionables or all those old-time Cherokee Bibles!"

Longarm said, "We both know what you gals have tucked away in your packsaddles, and that was the deal I made with them *rurales*. I made them see, or leastways I made their *sergeant* see, there was no easy way to hog the contents of them saddlebags unless we all just sort of rode out of his own officer's jurisdiction without him ever bothering to file a report on any gringo dead or alive."

Then a gun went off behind him, close, and Longarm whirled to see the other Fullbasket twin reel from her own saddle, an unfired Starr .32 whore pistol still clutched in her hand.

As Longarm moved without thinking to catch her as she fell off her horse, the churchgoing Alice Bluejacket, standing on her own feet with a smoking Winchester, yelled, "Look out!" and fired again in Longarm's general direction. But this time she blew the other twin off her own saddle in the opposite direction.

In the total confusion that followed, the brown-haired Alice told him, "I was watching them. Why weren't you watching them better? I thought you'd told me they'd already gotten two men killed over all that money!"

Longarm waved the others back, yelling, "Follow Chavez and leave us not forget Lot's wife! I'll tell you all about it on the ferry, if I ever get to the blamed ferry. I'll tidy up here as the rest of you beeline for the border, hear?"

So they rode out, single file, as Longarm tethered the four ponies the Fullbasket twins had chosen to a corral rail, leaving the twins ten yards apart in the dust for now. Little Alice Bluejacket joined him there, quietly murmuring, "Those Mexicans are coming."

Longarm turned to see his old pal, the *rurale* sergeant, rounding the corner with just his corporal. Longarm told the Cherokee gal, "You're stuck. You should have ridden on with the others. You're likely safer here with me and them ranking Mexicans for now."

The sergeant dismounted between the sprawled female corpses to scowl at Longarm and demand, "Is this how you deliver packsaddles whose owners are no longer under my captain's jurisdiction, *pendejo*?"

Longarm answered easily, "Since when would the natural deaths of two tourists who drank the water be a matter worth the time of *los rurales*? Doesn't everyone know that unfortunates who contract that *tifoideo* tend to ooze some blood and ought to be buried *poco tiempo*?"

The sergeant smiled, friendly as a turning shark, and decided, "We shall see who needs for to be buried around here after you show me the money, gringo!"

Longarm pointed at the tethered pack ponies and said, "Under some underwear and books. See for yourself. It's up to you whether you want to show anyone else, of course."

So in less than an hour Longarm and Alice Bluejacket were on their way after the others. But having an hour's start, the others had of course boarded an earlier ferry, and once Longarm and the Cherokee gal were on the far side, they found Chavez had blue-streaked for Fort Hancock as if he feared those *rurales* might cross over after him. As soon as you studied on what *his* rebel head would be worth to a Mexican bounty hunter, his skittishness made a certain sense.

Longarm, feeling surer they were safe, told Alice it was important he get off some wires and sit tight near the crossing until he got a few answers. He assured her she'd be safe riding on alone to see if she could catch up. But she said she felt safer with him, as horrid an old thing as he might be.

So with one thing and another, including supper by sundown at a sidewalk *cafetín* she found "so romantic," it was well after dark by the time he'd gotten answers to most of his wires, and it wasn't as tough as he'd expected to talk a church secretary, who wasn't a *preaching* woman for heaven's sake, into even more romance upstairs. Somehow, they never did seem to catch up with the main party before they got into El Paso to find they'd all lit out for the Indian Territory.

Longarm talked Alice, or maybe she talked him, into a last night at another hotel down the street from the Eagle. And parting really was sweet sorrow with Alice Bluejacket, for as experienced as she had to be, the little brown-haired Cherokee made love with a sort of shy innocence that put a man in mind of a bride on her honeymoon, and might have been the hope against hope that had lured many a poor simp into marrying up.

But since Alice had confided, their first night together, that she wasn't fixing to settle down until she'd seen some more of the world, Longarm felt comfortable as well as cuddly that last spring night of love.

Then it was morning and he put her on a train and turned to face the harsh light of another day, knowing they'd both get over it in time.

At the Western Union he found the answer to one long-shot wire he'd sent giving Western Union, El Paso, as his return address. Seeing that it confirmed one last suspicion, and seeing that he'd made a promise to another lady, Longarm ambled on over to the Baker place, arriving just before La Siesta, to find Fran Baker had made it home, all right, and her daddy was still out of town playing politics.

The blue-eyed brunette blushed becomingly and declared she hadn't been expecting company at that hour. He'd already notice her kimono of sky-blue Turkish toweling that matched her eyes. He offered to leave, but she hauled him up the stairs to her quarters, and rang for a servant as she sat him on a chaise near her dressing table. When her Mexican maid came in, Fran ordered a pitcher of iced sangria, and sat on the edge of her own four-poster as she demanded he keep his promise and tell her what on earth had been going on all that time.

Longarm said, "To begin with, you were right that something sneaky was going on, but Reverend Gibson and everyone else we rid south with were acting in good faith."

The white gal grimaced, and decided not to get into the Cherokee blonde and all that swimming in the Chihuahua desert. So Longarm just shrugged and said, "The really sneaky Cherokee were plotting flimflams down by the headwaters of the Rio Verde from before the beginning of our rescue expedition. Nobody really needed to be rescued. A handful of assimilated Christian Cherokee had been running a long-established mission to some Mexican Indians who spoke a dialect of Iroquoian and might have been distant kin to regular Cherokee. Their mission had been funded, up until the War betwixt the States, by a few rich white Southerners who might have felt some guilt about the Trail of Tears or might have just been idealistic. There's no way to ask 'em. They were all killed or just died by the time the war and the Reconstruction were over. So there's been no funding from the States, and the Indian hill farmers down yonder didn't have more than sweet smiles to offer. So the mission had to be shut down, save for a skeleton force of caretakers. One of the things they'd been left to take care of was a chest of church funds they'd accumulated."

Fran objected, "I thought you said they'd closed the mission when they couldn't get any more funding from the States."

Longarm said, "I'm coming to that. Church politics being as they are, even amongst us white folks, there was some confusion a slicker called Peter Redbird thought to use to his own advantage. As a lay member left to just guard the property, Redbird and his own clique wired other congregations in the States for help. Help in getting the fifty thousand in paper he'd dug up back to the States, that is. The Diaz dictatorship don't give toad squat about Catholics, Protestants, or the Great God Mumbo Jumbo as long as the government collects its Royal Eighth on all gold, silver, or other wealth leaving Mexico. That started as a royal Spanish notion. But no Mex government since has ever thought to repeal it."

The maid came in with the sangria and more nachos. Fran told her as she was leaving that they didn't want to be disturbed. As Fran turned back to Longarm, he told her, "Them two naughty Cherokee boys and their doxies, the Fullbasket twins, hoped to sneak fifty grand in paper out as reading material amid the confusion of a border-jumping rescue expedition. And it might have worked. We accepted them twins at face value. If they hadn't been greedy and wanted it *all,* the four of them would have joined us before we were halfway there, and we'd have carried them merrily back to Texas without ever passing through Mex customs. But the sneaky gals betrayed the sneaky boys, and so much for that part. The hard part would have been convicting the twins in any U.S. court of law for what they'd done. Even if an American judge and jury believed they'd turned those old boys in to the Mex police, those boys *were* trying to evade Mex law, and it would have been the *duty* of law-abiding tourist gals to turn them in, see?"

Fran didn't see. She said the Fullbasket twins had been two-faced little snips. Then she said, "Hold on, Custis. If those girls betrayed those boys to hog fifty thousand dollars they'd stolen from their own church, wouldn't that add up to grand larceny?"

Longarm said, "I was hoping it might. But I had my doubts, and in the end Miss Bluejacket sure saved us a heap of paperwork about all that paper money."

As she poured their cool wine punch she replied, "I noticed. Whatever happened to Miss Bluejacket, by the way, and won't you be in a little trouble for bribing those *rurales* with all those church funds that should have been returned to their rightful owners?"

Longarm reached for his glass as he calmly replied, "I just saw Miss Bluejacket off aboard a homeward-bound combination. As for that fifty thousand dollars in paper money, I don't think anyone but them *rurales* are likely to feel really vexed with me now. You see, what them thieving Cherokee had missed and what that greedy *rurale* sergeant missed, since none of them had much personal experience with the war, was that all them fifty-dollar notes were *Confederate money*, not worth the paper they'd been printed on."

Fran Baker laughed so hard she spilled sangria all over her kimono and had to take it off, or leastways, that was the excuse she gave as she lay back across her bedspread, naked as a jay.

So Longarm thought it best to set his own sangria aside and just remove his own duds neatly.

Watch for

**LONGARM AND THE GOLDEN GODDESS**

261$^{st}$ novel in the exciting LONGARM series
from Jove

*Coming in August!*